# MYSTIC EMBRACE

## BY

## CHARLOTTE BLACKWELL

**World Castle Publishing**
http://www.worldcastlepublishing.com

**World Castle Publishing**
Pensacola, Florida

Copyright © Charlotte Blackwell 2011
ISBN: 9781937085537
Library of Congress Catalogue Number 2011931981
First Edition World Castle Publishing November 1, 2011
http://www.worldcastlepublishing.com

**Licensing Notes**

Cover Artist: Karen Fuller
Photo from Shutterstock
Editor: Rhonda Klassen

# DEDICATION:

This is for both my wonderful grandmothers, who I miss dearly. You may not have wished to be supernatural, but you always had magickal powers to me. I love you and miss you both. Rest in peace, until we meet again.

Also a special thank you to my dear friends that have helped me so much along the way, Kathi Barton, Joann H. Buchanan, Mary Ting and Karen Fuller. Thank you for believing in me, pushing me and helping me to grow.

CHARLOTTE BLACKWELL

# ACKNOWLEDGEMENT:

The character Margret and "the twelve" were created by Mary Ting, author of Crossroads, and used with her permission and guidance. Thank you, Mary, for all your help and encouragement with this addition to my story line. I am so excited to have our characters cross-over.

# CHAPTER ONE
## On the Hunt

With everything that has happened in the past year it's hard to believe I'm somewhat sane. Finding out that my sister Eliza and I are *witches* and meeting a family of *vampires* is pretty unbelievable. Now, though, we have to concentrate on our own problems since the rogue *vampires* that we fought recently have somewhat been neutralized. We live everyday with the certainty that the demon Naberius is searching for us, as we are searching for him. On the lookout all the time, Eliza and I must proceed with caution and remain alert at all times. We only found out we were *witches* last year, but have already learned so much and our powers are growing fast.

Today we're on a mission to hunt down the *demon* that killed our parents so many years ago, when I was just a baby. Walking through the dark underworld, I attempt to get my bearings, noticing the rock that's surrounding me. It's cave-like, cold, and damp with a heavy musty, mildew odor that induces my gag reflex. A bright red glow, similar to a tail light on a car, is ahead of us and helps to light our way. The rough rock tunnel has various shapes, protruding from and trapped within the walls, somewhat resembling some kind of beings; maybe a metaphor for trapped souls, or possibly real souls. Shivers run down my spine at the thought, wondering who they could be. In the past year, since we've gained our powers, we helped our friends the Pierces and focused on our training, preparing for this day. Over the last few months Eliza and I easily defeated the last set of low ranking *demons* including Arioch, the *demon* of vengeance, which Naberius sent for us. Thanks to the information we retrieved from the previous *demons* we have been able to find the realm where his lair is. After traveling through several different realms, we believe this is it.

Exploring the underworld and looking for the one that took our parents from us, I can't help but feel we're in over our heads, but decide to keep my insecurities to myself. Grams told us Naberius is the *demon* who attacked our parents that day, nearly seventeen years ago, soon after my birth. He wanted us then, and when our parents wouldn't allow it, he took them. If it weren't for the protection and power-binding spell that our mom was able to put on us right before her demise, he would have gotten to us. Now, with our powers back, we're here to face him, *witch* against *demon,* and we refuse to lose— losing would be worse than death. My nerves and unease begin to dissipate. I'm not as light headed as when we first arrived here; crossing through the astral planes always makes me feel funny—kinda light headed, like I'm floating, but I'm getting used to it. Eliza's power to control time has evolved to astral projection; she now can manipulate time and space, which has brought us here on yet another unknown journey. When she holds my hand, Eliza has the ability to bring me with her. It is usually best to lie down and meditate. Our bodies begin to feel a pull and just like that we are gone. Our physical bodies remain still, alive where we left them, and our astral bodies also appear to be alive elsewhere. I'm telekinetic but I can't astral project on my own; maybe one day I will learn. Eliza's powers have strengthened so fast; at first she could only project herself.

My telekinetic powers, the ability to move things with my mind, helps when surprises pop up. I first found out about my power last year at school. I had no idea I was able to move things with my mind until the day Mel, the bully that she is, cornered me at school. My blood boiled and the energy from all around me pulsated through my being. The lockers flew open and the halls became littered with pens and papers; everything swirled around me. I think I was more terrified than her. Thank God for Matt–his rushing in and hurrying me back to Grams place saved me. Everything became clearer then and I found out I was a *witch*, a Magnificent One. My sister and I are descendents of the great Salem *witches*, and we were both born on the sixth day of the month at midnight–the witching hour. We inherited great power from all the *witches* before us, and are meant to help fight evil and protect the innocent. But before we can truly do that, we need to take care of this old business and clear our heads.

"I really think this is the right one, Ebony. Just like Arioch described it. I can see the trapped souls within the rock walls. I just never knew it would be so literal," Eliza says with anxious anticipation.

"You know, I was thinking the same thing, but I didn't realize that he mentioned the trapped souls. Either way though, I agree this may be the right spot. I'm so ready for this. I can't believe after all this time we get to avenge Mom and Dad's death." I confirm my excitement and release some of my anxiety.

Little by little, the red light ahead of us dims and begins to flicker until it is completely off; in its place, a bright white light emerges in its place. Two figures appear before us: one man and one woman. Eliza and I both stop. *Could these be demon warriors?* I wonder, but then my thoughts turn to the *Book of Shadows*. I remember reading 'a *spirit guide* can appear to a *witch* in human form, following a bright white light'.

"Eliza, did you ever read in the *Book of Shadows* about *spirit guides*?"

"In fact, now that you mention it Ebony, I did. Do you think these could be our spirit guides?"

"Why now? We haven't had a *spirit guide* or a *guardian* contact us yet. I don't understand. I think we should talk to Matt, when we get back to the manor of course."

I love that my boyfriend Matt knows so much about *witches* and the supernatural from his training. What I don't like is the fact that he is training to be a *guardian*. Every witch is supposed to have a guardian. It makes it hard because Eliza and I don't have one yet. I mean really, why don't we? We are The Magnificent Ones, after all. I just don't want to lose Matt to some other *witch*. Becoming a *guardian* is in his blood; his grandfather was one and is now a Great One, a leader of the *guardians*. What concerns me is with Matt in training it only means one thing; inevitable death. He has to die to complete his training and become a full *guardian*. I'm so grateful to have Matt in my life; I love him to pieces, and having him help us so much is amazing. His family history of *guardians* is what has made him a chosen one, an *angel* of sorts for *witches*. His training began shortly after his birth, and although he has a vast amount of knowledge, he won't gain any active powers until he dies. I really hope that doesn't happen for a long time–he means the world to me and I need his help still. When my powers started to appear, he saved me from the ridicule at school and helped me through the change, and I didn't even know that he was a *guardian* yet. Needing to get my head back in the game, I shake off my thoughts of the man waiting for me back home and return to the cave we have been wandering through.

We move towards the white figures with caution. As we get closer I sense a feeling of familiarity and comfort radiating from them. The woman is nearly translucent; she is wearing a long white flowing gown and her dark skin is as smooth as milk chocolate. Her lips part as if preparing to speak and then we hear a whisper from her.

"My beautiful girls, return home! He is waiting for you and you are not prepared for this fight yet."

"Mom, Dad, is that you?" Eliza questions with a slight tremble in her voice.

"Yes my dear, we have never left you, but you must turn back now. We have been given permission to appear to you and assist you in learning the craft. It is much safer for us and for you at the manor. Please return now," responds the man, our father.

We both recognize them from the pictures we've seen of our parents. Grams always ensures we know how much they loved us, and keeps pictures out at all times. From what we've been told about our parents, Mom was a *witch* and Dad a mortal. I guess he must have had a little magick in him after all, in order to be here and appear to us now. I try to withhold my emotions, but seeing my parents for the first time and hearing them speak to me is more over-whelming than I could ever imagine. My heart begins pounding so hard I think my chest may rip open. Tears well up in my eyes with a slight burn, and I try to fight them back.

🝆 🝆 🝆

At their request, Eliza at once pulls us back; we return to our physical bodies at the manor. Nausea over takes me–the quick return is difficult to adjust to. As I look around I see Grams, Matt, and Sophia all waiting with trepidation. Sophia is my best friend and a *vampire*; we met last year at school. After seeing her day crystal, I knew she was one of the *vampires* that my Grams had helped years ago. She is well over 100 years old, but aside from her vast knowledge, you would never guess it. Sophia is immortally seventeen. Our families are very close and help one another in dealing with supernatural threats. Right now, it's our threat; Grams rushes over and cover us with blankets. Astral travel always gives us a lower body temperature. We take a few minutes to collect our thoughts and ground ourselves and then we both take a quick look around to see if our mom and dad returned here with us.

"What's the matter Ebony, who are you looking for? We're all right here with you, you're safe," Matt says in a comforting tone.

Grams takes a seat at the end of the bed. "You saw them. They came to you, didn't they?"

"How...how did you know?" I ask with surprise.

"I've always sensed your mother and father with us. I know they are your *spirit guides*. There is no one better to guide you to the light than your own parents," she admits.

With tears welling in her eyes, Eliza asks, "Why wouldn't you tell us?"

"I didn't tell you because this is something you needed to find out when your parents felt it was the right time. They without a doubt felt it was the right time now, that this is when you need them the most."

"We understand; this is just a little bit of a shock." I sit up to hug her.

"Okay, someone needs to fill me in. I thought your parents were dead, what are spirit guides?" Sophia asks with confusion.

Matt smiles. "Let me explain this one. Everyone has something called a *spirit guide*. It is that little voice inside of a mortals head. With *witches* or those with physic abilities, *spirit guides* can appear or communicate freely with them. They do require permission to make initial contact with their entity. This is what's happened to Ebony and Eliza. They're at a time in their lives that without the guidance of their *spirit guide* there could be a shift in the universal order. Because of the power they hold and the way their parents died, it only makes sense that their parents be their guides," Matt explains.

Matt is always so good at explaining witchcraft. He's helped us learn so much since we came of age last year and regained our powers that were once hidden from not only us, but those who threaten us. I'm lucky to have Matt in my life; his support and love holds me together. The knowledge he has gained from his years of *guardian* training has also been a great help to my sister and me. I try not to think about the day I will lose him and he becomes a *guardian*, otherwise known as an angel guide for other *witches*, but it can be hard at times. I do know he has to procreate before he is taken; the *guardians* pass along their gifts through genetics. Knowing this is what gives me hope and the knowledge that I do have some time before he leaves me.

"Yeah that helps a little, thanks Matt," Sophia says.

"So girls, what did your parents say to you?" Grams asks with excitement.

"Just that now is not the time to take on Naberius. He is aware of our coming and we need to prepare more. They promised to help us with our training," Eliza explains.

"I must say that I agree. I'm not ready to lose you Ebony. Naberius is the protector to the gates of hell. He's a strong *demon* and in charge of twenty nine legions, a Marquis of hell. You and your sister have the power to defeat him, but you must be prepared for a bigger battle than you could ever imagine. This is a magick fight and you won't have the Pierces or the Williams to help you. One or both of you may get hurt and it's not just one demon, but many that may come before and even after Naberius. I'll work with you, and teach you all I know. Sophia, he's even been associated with the Cerberus," Matt asserts.

I can't help but reflect on the Cerberus, a group of rogue *vampires* we fought this past winter. Combining our powers with the Pierce *vampires* (Sophia's family), the *shape shifters* we met that protect the area, and the governing *vampires,* the Renata leaders of the *vampires,* we were able to stop them. Thanks to Caspian, Sophia's brother, we learned that the Cerberus plan to gain power from the area so they can overtake the Renata. It has been a while since we have heard much from them in that sense, but Caspian is still working on it. I just hope they can wait till Eliza and I deal with our own demons.

I reach for Matt's hand, "Thank you Matt, we'll make sure we're prepared and until that time we deal with whatever scum he throws at us. I'm not ready to lose you either. I love you all. You mentioned he is associated with the Cerberus; just keep in mind that we helped Sophia's family defeat them back in January. At least we thought we did, until we learned about Cyrus and Drake."

"They shouldn't cause much trouble, but remember there're always more of them. Cyrus and Drake have already proved that."

I find myself thinking back to last year, when I first met Sophia in Spanish class. The moment I saw her necklace, I knew all of Grams tales were true. I was scared and excited all at once. *Vampires* existed and with the help of *witches* they could become day walkers, and Sophia was one of them. Her necklace is made with a special day crystal, a black diamond called *veneficus lamia sol solis partonus*, which is Latin for "magickal *vampire* sun protector", blessed by powerful witches–my Grams and her mother.

Sophia lives with a family of *vampires*, the Pierce family; they've been living civilly for nearly three quarters of a century, and I'm lucky to call them my friends. Each member of her family has a talisman, with the exception of Caspian who returned his. When rogue *vampires* threatened our small town of Wenham, we managed to destroy them with the assistance of the native *shape shifters* and now our friends, the Williams, and the Pierce family. However, since then we have learned that there are always more where they came from.

"Well, I think it is time for the girls to get some rest. We can work on training tomorrow," Grams insists.

Matt and Sophia lean in one at a time giving both Eliza and I hugs. Matt takes mine one step further, with a slight touch; he brushes a stray strand of hair from my face and brushes his lips against mine. Pulling him closer to me, I move my lips in sync with his and take in the full robust aroma of his breath, tasting the mint Trident gum he's been chewing. He instantly energizes me with his touch. Grams comes back with some tea for me and Eliza. Matt and Sophia take their cue and leave through the large oak door. The roar of Sophia's car echo's through the house as she peels out of the driveway. I take the tea from Grams, lifting the cup to my mouth and gently blowing at the steaming liquid before taking a sip.

CHARLOTTE BLACKWELL

# CHAPTER TWO
## Hints

Waking at first light, I feel well rested and ready to train as I crawl out of bed and pull back the large green drapes to my room, allowing the light to come in. Basking in the sun of a new day, the brightness beams in proving to be full of energy and filling me with optimism. I'm glad we still have a few weeks left to summer break, and hope to enjoy some of this beautiful weather with my friends. Deciding to let Eliza sleep in I head downstairs to the office. I want to study more on alternate realms and the various *demons* we have faced. I wonder if there is a pattern to the attacks Naberius has sent to us. Looking at the large leather bound book and tracing the outline of the triquetra, I feel a sense of relief within the three intertwining ovals; these represent my sister and me and the power we create together. I still find it amazing. As I flip through the *Book of Shadows*, I realize there is a new entry, one that was not there before. Our *Book of Shadows* has been handed down through generations of our family, and helps us to understand our roles as The Magnificent Ones; the world's most powerful *witches*. Magnificent Ones are always born on the sixth of the month at midnight, the witching hour, just like my sister and me. Our *Book of Shadows* is packed full of information about various supernatural forces, spells, potions and rituals, everything we need to be successful at protecting the innocent. I know that neither Eliza nor I put this new entry there because we always make our entries together and only when a circle is cast.

I assume my parents added it last night. "When one is traveling to alternate realms and through the pathways of the underworld there are rules to follow. Always be respectful of the *guards*; they will not cause you harm unless harm is caused to them or to their realm. You must never approach them or speak to them as they foresee that as a threat. When in alternate realms always remember the path you have taken, or you may become a trapped soul. Whichever way you go in is the way you must come out. Leaving through a different route leaves the gateways open to unwanted guests and negative energies will attach to you. After your travels always ensure proper grounding of yourself and return the energy to the realm, or there will be repercussions."

Maybe everyone is right–maybe we aren't ready for this yet. I have zero understanding about the underworld and travels through it. This must be what my parents want us to study today. I try to retrace our steps from last night. Did we follow the same path in? We must have. I don't recall seeing a split in the path. I pick up my sketchbook and a pencil, and begin to draw what I remember from our travels; we can add it to the *Book of*

*Shadows* later today. I'm not a good artist; maybe I should describe it to Sophia and have her do a sketch. Sophia is an amazing artist; no, Sophia is amazing at everything. I just wish she wouldn't always be so hard on herself.

The smell of vanilla and waffles comes wafting in from the kitchen. Closing the large leather hand bound *Book of Shadows* and placing it under my arm I follow the divine scent. I'll help set the table for breakfast and show Grams what I found this morning in the *Book of Shadows*. Grams may have something to add to Mom and Dad's entry. Heavy footsteps thump down the staircase as Eliza joins us in the kitchen. Her bright pink and very fuzzy housecoat is wrapped tightly around her tall, thin frame as she plops down in a chair. Eliza's thick black hair springs out in every direction, and she tries to pat down her nappy locks.

Still half asleep, Eliza asks, "Is that waffles I smell?"

"Yes it is. Waffles have always been the easiest way to get you out of bed," Grams admits with a chuckle.

"You spoil me, Grams," Eliza smiles.

"Well, that is what Grandmas are for my dear."

I pour each of us a glass of fresh squeezed orange juice into three large tumblers, as Gram's places the plate of homemade waffles on the table next to the fresh cream and berries and takes a seat.

"So when I woke up today, I decided to start on my studies while Eliza slept."

Grams pats my knee. "That is great Ebony, but do not get ahead of yourself."

21

"Don't worry Grams, I got the message loud and clear."

"What do you mean? Did Mom and Dad come back when I was sleeping?" Eliza asks with excitement.

"I think they were here when we were all sleeping. I found a message in our *Book of Shadows*," I explain.

"What does it say?" Eliza inquires.

"It explains about alternate realm travel," I go into detail and show them the entry. "I think we have a lot to learn still. Don't you?"

"It appears that way. I never knew it could be so dangerous. I knew about taking the same path in and out, but never the ramifications of not doing so," Eliza admits.

"Well, girls, once you're finished eating, why don't you go study and I will clean up breakfast today?"

"Thanks Grams, you're the best," we both say.

After we finish eating, we head back to the office and begin to peruse our notes, when we suddenly hear a bang. We move slowly and carefully towards the noise. I peer around the office to see if anything is different, and notice a book on the floor. It is open to a page about underworlds. Mom and Dad must be behind this. Grams comes running, as fast as a woman her age can run that is, to check on the noise as well.

"Everything is okay Grams; it was just a book from the shelf," I explain.

She nods and turns back to the kitchen. Eliza and I sit on the area rug of the floor next to the book and begin to take more notes.

About one o'clock the doorbell rings, "Ebony, Matt is here," Grams calls out.

"Can you send him in here please?"

I get up off the floor to greet Matt and notice that he has an armful of books and journals. "Hi there, handsome. Whatcha got?"

"These are just some of my study journals and texts for my *guardian* training. I thought they may help you."

"Thanks, we need all the help we can get." I take the books and journals, placing them on the floor where we are studying, and wrap my arms around him.

"I got permission from the Great Ones to help you and share our information with you. They agreed, based on the fact that your work is for the greater good.

"Please thank them for us. The support of the Great Ones is appreciated. I only wish we knew our *guardian*," Eliza declares.

"You will when the time is right. I'm sure he or she is watching out for you and you don't even realize it yet."

Now is a great time for a break. We have been cramped up on the floor for hours. So the three of us decide it's time to go meet Sophia, Nathanial and Luke at the pool hall. We have a great group of friends. Nathanial–Sophia's boyfriend and the best quarterback this town has ever seen–and his older brother Luke, who attends Harvard on a basketball scholarship and now is Eliza's boyfriend. They come from the most upstanding family. Nathanial knows about us being *witches* and our

23

powers; he also knows about the Pierce family being *vampires* and has never judged any of us. Even with how accepting Nathanial has been, we have not shared our secret with Luke. I can see how it has been weighing on Eliza and am grateful everyday that I decided to have full disclosure with Matt. Opening up to Matt made it so that, in turn, he opened up to me about being a future *guardian*. Since then he has taught Eliza and me so much about being *witches* and about our heritage.

"I can't wait to see Luke. It has only been a few days but I miss him so much," Eliza gushes.

"I am so glad you and Luke found one another. You really are perfect together," I give her a little nudge.

"I know it too. Let's go get our things and check on Grams before we leave."

Walking down the hall to the kitchen, we can see Grams sitting in one of the dining room chairs. She's stiff and something just doesn't seem right. Grams looks frozen; she doesn't move, but her eyes shift slightly. My heart sinks with fear that she is ill, maybe a stroke, or…*Oh God another demon attack*, I realize by the sulfur smell as I get closer to the kitchen. I don't think *demons* realize the stench they have.

"Someone or something is here. Matt I think you should leave and fast," I whisper with the softest voice.

Matt nods and quietly exits the manor. Eliza reaches to the apothecary cabinet for some potions we made earlier this week, notifying me that she has had the same realization as I have. I can see a figure in the mirror of the china cabinet, with a slight tilt of my head I direct

Eliza to enter from the other side. She hands me a trapping potion and we prepare to enter the kitchen area.

Slowly proceeding, I can hear Alexander in my head. 'Ebony, we are outside. Matt called us, Sophia, Mati and I got here as fast as we could. I'll stay connected and we're ready to help at the first sign of trouble.'

Alexander is Sophia's twin brother; he was Embraced, or turned, trying to save her. He has the ability to connect to others thoughts, telepathically, but much more advanced than just that. He can control whose thoughts he joins and whom he shares with. This power comes in very handy at times like this, when we are in trouble, like now.

'Thanks Alex, it has Grams so we have to be careful not to startle it.'

CHARLOTTE BLACKWELL

# CHAPTER THREE
## The Light

As I enter the kitchen, I pretend as if nothing is out of place. "Hey Grams, Eliza and I are going to meet up with the gang. She is just upstairs getting ready," I pretend.

Grams doesn't move, just as I suspected. Leaning over her, still trying to fool whatever has trapped her. "Grams, are you alright? Should I call an ambulance?" I give her arm a little shake. That's the sign for Eliza to enter.

She enters in silence; I stand and turn to face the *demon* in front of me. He doesn't notice Eliza come in, and just as fast as she pulled us out of the astral realm last night, she throws a power-diminishing potion. I follow it with the trapping potion, throwing underhand with near perfect precision.

With immense reflexes, he quickly throws a fireball at us but it bounces off the trap only to rebound back at him. Eliza only just misses hitting him with the power-diminishing spell, which means he is able to use his powers still. This changes things. We won't have much time before he can break through the trap and fully attack us. I scream in my head for Alexander to get Matt to bring me the *Book of Shadows*, knowing that he and Sophia can't touch it, due to the magick it holds and how it is protected. I hope that because Matt is a *guardian* in training, the book will allow him access. The *demon* continues to pitch fireballs at us. I work hard to deflect them with my telekinetic powers before they hit the trap and weaken it.

Within minutes Matt comes running with the book.

"Stop!" I scream, "Don't come in here, just throw it to me." I don't want the *demon* to get a look at Matt or get him in his sight. I don't know what other powers he has and if he can harm Matt with his mind or eyes.

"Be careful," he replies as he tosses the *Book of Shadows* to me.

Eliza grabs it and searches for an appropriate banishing spell, as I continue to deflect the fireballs back towards the demon. As soon as we banish him, the effects on Grams should reverse–I hope.

"I got it!" Eliza holds the book open so we can recite the chant.

We hold hands and chant,
"He who is evil,
Here to cause harm,
Return to your realm,
And forever be gone.
By the power in we,
So mote it be,
So mote it be,

28

So mote it be.

Moving as fast as we can, we cover Grams to protect her as the flames erupt on the demon, causing him to explode. I close my eyes, feeling the heat rush over us. The moment the heat retracts I look around the room to ensure everyone is alright. The flames and smoke get sucked into the ground like a whirlpool and then everything appears to return to normal again.

"He's gone! Is everyone okay?" I look for Matt; he peeks from the other room and I nod, signaling it's safe to enter.

Eliza answers with a slight shake in her voice, "Yeah, we're okay."

I notice Alexander and Sophia near the front door. They both check the scene to ensure we are all here. Matt and our *vampire* friends must have decided to stay a little closer than we expected.

"Grams, Grams, are you okay?" I give her a little shake her head flops forwards and her eyes remain fixed on the spot where the *demon* was. The air trapped in my lungs begins to burn, and I can't take in any more air. With panic setting in, my heart pounds harder with every passing second and I have to fight the urge to vomit.

"Sophia, help! She isn't waking up. What happened? When we banished him, the trance should have been broken. Please help her." I beg as the tears stream down my face.

Sophia has the amazing power to heal others that are near death or hurt, although she can't heal the dead; once the life force has left all bets are off.

I gently lay Grams on the floor as Sophia rushes over to heal her. With Grams head in my lap and Eliza hanging on to her hand, Sophia kneels next to us. Her hands calmly run over Grams body and stop over her heart. Sophia lowers her head in concentration. I can feel the healing energy radiating from her, and I pray to the almighty deity to save Grams.

Sophia lifts her head, "Ebony, I am so sorry. There is nothing I can do for her; her life force is gone. It was a heart attack."

I lean in to Grams, "NO! You can't leave us, Grams. We are not ready yet." Grams has cared for us since Mom and Dad passed away. She is all Eliza and I have in this world.

Eliza sits back in shock, and I lean over towards her. Wrapping my arms around her we both sob. Matt runs over and holds both of us. His uncanny gift to give peace and bring calm is proving very helpful now. Through tear hazed eyes I see a soft white light appear over Grams. Watching as her spirit enters the light, I see her as she turns and smiles. This is it. Eliza and I are alone to face the world, and all the evils in the world, with no guidance.

Alexander moves quietly into the other room with the phone in his hand. Three beeps echo through the house as he dials 911 reporting Grams death. I continue to go over the events in my head, concerned that we may have done something wrong. Could we have caused this? Could we have caused Grams to die? It isn't long before the ambulance arrives and the medics officially call the time of death. We watch as they load Grams into the ambulance.

With a very empathetic tone, one of the medics explains, "We'll be taking the body to Wenham General. Dr. Pierce is there waiting for our arrival. She will examine your grandmother and be available to answer any questions you may have. Do you have a ride to the hospital?"

"Yes, I'll bring them," Matt speaks up.

Sophia's Aunt Constance and Uncle Isaac are both doctors at the hospital. It comes in handy having them work in the emergency department when a supernatural issue arises. Isaac isn't just a doctor, but also a hematologist; it makes it easy for him to acquire blood for the Pierce family. He's also working on creating a synthetic blood for them to use for feeding and even for the medical community to use.

As we follow the ambulance to the hospital, I continue to go over things in my head. I can't believe that Grams is gone or that Eliza and I are going to help save the world without her. Alexander drives us to the hospital so Matt can stay close to Eliza and me in the back seat. Matt's ability to calm us makes it possible to think clearly. Sophia has already called her family, and they will meet us at the hospital. This is all so surreal. First our parent's spirits came to us, and then we banish a *demon* in the kitchen, only to lose Grams in the end. This is way too much for anyone to handle.

Pulling up to the hospital, Luke is already outside waiting to help support Eliza. Matt helps me inside; and

Constance, or should I say Dr. Pierce, is also there waiting for us.

She wraps her arms around us in a loving embrace, "Girls, I am so sorry. You know our family will always be here for you, and we'll help you get through this. I'll take you guys to the family room; Florence, Elijah and the rest of my family are already in there waiting for you. I still need to do an examination on your grandmother, and then I'll be back in to talk with you."

In the family room, we have all of those who mean the most to us here. The entire Pierce family, Nathanial and Luke McCord, and of course Matt, are all here to help us through this surreal loss. I realize that these people standing before me are the only family Eliza and I have and I am so grateful to have them all in our lives. We all sit in silence remembering Grams while we wait for Constance to return. The door slowly creaks open and Constance finds herself looking at an incredibly somber crowd looking to her for answers. "Eliza, Ebony, I've completed the exam on Ms. Edwina and in my medical opinion I believe Sophia was right. Your grandmother died from a myocardial infarction, also known as an MI or heart attack. There is nothing you could have done; her age alone increased her risk. A postmortem blood workup proves that she also had high blood pressure and cholesterol issues. She was a wonderful woman and lived a wonderful life. You girls meant everything to her, and she has always been extremely proud of you. Knowing your grandmother, no matter what happened she wouldn't have left you if she didn't think you were ready."

Tears stream down every face in the room and each and every one of us nods in agreement.

"I need to know if you girls would like me to do an autopsy. This can give us absolute proof of what your grandmother died from," Constance informs us.

Isaac stands up next to Constance, "Do you girls know much about autopsies? Would you like one of us to explain them to you?"

Eliza looks up and says, "No, I think we both have a basic understanding of what it entails. I would like to know if anyone in this room thinks that we need to do an autopsy."

"I don't want to Eliza. I can't stand the thought of them cutting Grams up. We can't disrespect her that way."

"Ebony, it's done in a very respectful manner. If that is what you are worried about, I assure you, you do not need to concern yourself. I would even be willing to assist if it makes you feel better," Isaac comforts.

"I don't think it's necessary, I trust Constance and her medical opinion. The fact that Sophia was so close when it happened and attempted healing her is enough for me." I say this without even thinking of Luke and him not knowing our secret. Eliza gives me a slight glare and I try to cover my tracks. "I mean Sophia did her best with CPR–you've trained her well. Doing an autopsy on Grams won't change anything."

"I agree," says Eliza, "Grams is gone and there is nothing that you can do to that will change that," Eliza rationalizes.

# CHAPTER FOUR
## Next Step

We go back to the manor to collect a few necessary items. Florence has invited us to stay with them for as long as we need. Eliza and I agree that is exactly what we need right now; neither of us wants to go back home right now. Even just going back to pack some bags proves to be difficult. Getting out of the car and up the front step feels like the longest walk I've ever taken. Both Eliza and I stop at the front door, frozen like statues. Sophia, Alexander and Matt are with us; the rest went to the Pierce house to set up for our arrival. It was difficult to talk Luke into going without Eliza, but we aren't ready for him to stumble on any remnants from the *demon*.

"Would you like to go back to the car? I can pack your bags for you, at least for tonight and tomorrow," Sophia offers.

"Thanks Sophia, but we're going to have to go in sooner or later. I think it is best if we just get this over with. The first time is going to be bad no matter when we do it," I respond.

Once inside, neither of us looks towards the kitchen as our eyes fill with tears. We both go to our rooms and pack our bags in less than five minutes. Hurrying back down the stairs with a need to get out of this house as fast as possible, I trip, rolling down at least ten stairs before landing at the bottom. A loud snapping sound, like a lonely twig on the forest floor snapping in half, echo's through the corridor, and I scream in pain.

"My God, Ebony are you okay?" Matt runs to my aid.

"God, it hurts so bad. I think I broke something."

At the sound of my cries, Sophia runs to my side, "Don't move Ebony—your ankle is broken. I'm going to put my hands around it and it may hurt more from my touch, but I promise it won't take long to be as good as new."

Excruciating pain shoots through my entire leg as Sophia grabs a hold of my ankle. In one swift motion, she turns my ankle to its original place. It feels as though somebody is chopping—no ripping—my entire foot off. I bellow so loud that the windows in the house shake as my voice cracks with the pain. Then suddenly, I begin to feel warmth over my ankle. Sophia is next to me, deep in meditation and concentration. She is the best healer I ever met (okay, the only healer) and the best friend a girl could ask for. Warmth moves up my leg in ripples; I can feel the healing of bone rejoining. I only wish Sophia could heal me from the pain of losing Grams.

Sophia sits up and nods to Matt, and he scoops me up in one quick but gentle motion and carries me back to the car. I notice Eliza grabs my bag as she walks out of the manor. I wish our parents would reappear to us–I would love to know that Grams is okay and with them now.

♦ ♦ ♦

Back at the Pierce household, arrangements for Grams' funeral are already being made. Florence and Elijah are helping to take care of all the details. Florence makes arrangements for the obituary for the morning paper, and Elijah contacts the funeral home to set up the service. We don't have any other family so there's no one to call. I'll have to look in the *Book of Shadows* to ensure we do the proper ceremony to see Grams off to the spirit realm. That will have to wait until tomorrow though. I am mentally and physically exhausted and just need to get some rest.

"Eliza, Ebony, the guest rooms are all set up for you and Alexander has already taken your belongings up. You know that we consider you both our family. I have the fridge stocked with everything you may like; please help yourself or even just ask and we will get it for you. Our entire family is here for you, and we will help you get through this. We can continue to take care of all the arrangements for you if you would like." Florence hugs both of us and then offers us a cup of tea.

"Thank you so much, Florence–I'm so glad that we're not alone. Do you mind if we take our tea upstairs and go to bed?" Eliza asks.

"Not at all my dear. We've also spoken to Matt and Luke's families. The boys will also be staying here tonight, in case you need them. They will be just down the hall from you."

With a smile, Luke says, "Thank you Mrs. Pierce. We appreciate it."

"No need for formalities, we are all family here. It is just Florence, please."

Sophia shows us to our rooms Alexander already has our pajamas laid on the bed and covers turned down. He has also left fresh towels for us to shower, and has put all our toiletries in the washroom. This family is so incredibly thoughtful and caring; no one would ever believe they are *vampires*. We take turns in the shower and getting ready for bed. I notice Matilda putting some calming music on the stereo and placing books beside our beds. Matt is waiting in my room when I get out of the washroom.

"Hey beautiful, I just wanted to tuck you into bed and make sure you are okay."

"Thanks, Matt. I think I'm doing better now. I still can't believe that Grams is gone."

"I understand; everything happened without any warning and I can only imagine how it is tearing you apart. Just know that I'm here for you, and that your Grams loved you very much."

"I know, she was a wonderful woman. She raised Eliza and me from the beginning. We never had our parents around, all we ever had was her...and now we don't. What are we ever going to do without her?"

"I know it'll be difficult, but I know you can do it. Your grandmother didn't raise any idiots. Try not to worry about it right now. It'll be easier to deal with once you get some rest."

"You may be right. Will you lie with me, until I fall asleep?"

"Of course I will. I'll do anything for you."

Crawling into bed next to me, Matt pulls up the blankets and wraps his arms around me in a loving embrace. I've been so lucky to have him in my life. He's supported me since day one, even when I tried to push him away after finding out I was *witch*. He's always been so understanding and supportive of my friendship with *vampires,* and was even open and honest enough with me about his *guardian* training. I bury my head deeper into his chest, realizing how lucky I truly am to have him in my life. Matt leans down and kisses my forehead. With a slight smile I look up at him, slowly moving towards him for a soft gentle kiss.

"I love you Matt. Thank you for being here for me," I whisper with a soft sincere tone.

"Ebony, I couldn't love anyone more than you."

He lightly runs his hands through my hair and places them on either side of my face with a passionate look, then kisses me again. Pulling myself closer to him and moving up slightly, leaning on one elbow, I place one hand on his cheek, rubbing his ear lobe between my thumb and index finger. We begin kissing each other, more passionately than ever. He slowly runs his hands down my back. I get up onto my knees in front of him. He pulls himself up to the sitting position, and I climb on his lap. He begins to kiss my neck and moves his hands up the back of my shirt on my bare skin. I reach down, grabbing his shirt and pull it up over his head. With a slight push back, I kiss his lips then take my time and move with gentle passion to his neck. Running my hands over his bare chest, I kiss my way down to his navel.

"Ebony, I want this more than anything, but are you sure this is the right time?" he says as he pulls me up towards him.

"Matt, there is nothing more that I want right now. We have been together for almost a year now. We've been through more than most couples, and we have gotten through it. I feel so calm and relaxed right now and feel that it is time for us to finally make love."

"I just want to make sure that it is not my ability to calm people that is making you feel this way right now."

"This is me, wanting to make love to the man of my dreams." I lean down and kiss him again, and then fearlessness takes over and I sit back up and slide my shirt off.

With a slight gasp he wraps his arms around me and flips me onto my back. Little by little, he kisses me and caresses me, with the most loving touch I have ever felt. Taking our time we enjoy every inch of each other's bodies and every moment we are sharing together with pure gentle love. The remaining clothes soar through the air towards the floor as the passion between us rises.

◆ ◆ ◆

"That was amazing. I'm so glad we got to experience our first time, together," I whisper.

"Ebony, you are the kindest, most beautiful woman I've ever known, and I want to be with you forever. I promise never to leave you and always to be here for you. Thank you so much for allowing me to share your life."

The tears slowly stream down my face. He is the sweetest most articulate man; who could ask for anything more?

"Honey, is everything okay?" he asks with sincere concern.

"Yeah, this has just been a very emotional day. First the *demon*, then Grams, and now we make love for the first time and you say the sweetest, most amazing things. These are not all bad tears. There are sad and happy tears here, and it is only because of you that there are happy tears. Thank you for just being you, and thank you for loving me."

We lay in each other's arms for quite a while. I'm almost asleep when Matt says, "I better go to my room. If you need me, I'm just across the hall. I love you and I'll see you in the morning. Try and have a good sleep."

"Goodnight. I love you too, and thank you for everything." I give him one last kiss and slowly drift off to sleep.

CHARLOTTE BLACKWELL

# CHAPTER FIVE
**Spirit Visions**

As I fall asleep I am more aware of myself and my surroundings than ever before. Tonight feels different. My entire body feels relaxed and light, as if I could float away. Even once I'm asleep, I still feel very aware. Letting myself go in my dreams, I begin to walk along a dark tunnel with many branching pathways. With a sense of someone calling my name I continue down the long straight path ahead of me as if I'm being pulled. It's not long before I see Eliza next to me.

She smiles and says, 'This is the weirdest dream I've ever had'.

'Weirdest dream you've had? I thought this was *my* dream. Is it possible that we connected telepathically and are having the same dream?' I say with surprise.

The same bright light we saw when we first saw Mom and Dad appears in front of us. The excitement of seeing them again is palpable. But this time we only notice one figure in front of us. Once the figure becomes clearer to us, we realize it's Grams. My heart leaps with excitement.

In her kind and gentle tone she says, "I am so glad you both heard my call and came. I am so sorry to have left you so unexpectedly, but I know that you are both strong enough to continue your journey and help in the fight against evil."

"How is this possible Grams? How can Eliza and I both be having the same dream?"

"This is not a dream, my love. This is what they call an out-of-body-experience. It is similar to Eliza's astral-projection. Your bodies appear to be sleeping, but your spirit has entered the sacred spirit realm. Here you are able to learn and speak to your ancestors."

"So when we saw Mom and Dad earlier–is this where we were?" Eliza inquires.

"No sweetheart, they came to you in *spirit* form. We *spirits* can sometimes gain permission from the higher power to visit our loved ones when they need us. That is what your parents did. Now that you have been led to the spirit realm you will be able to talk to us almost anytime you need to," she explains.

"And exactly how do we do that?" I ask.

"It's quite simple," Grams begins.

We continue for what seems like hours, with Grams teaching me how to meditate and guiding me. Serenity washes over me as I exhale and release the events of the past couple of days–no, the past few months. Grams shows me that once in a meditative state I just think about who I wish to talk to that has passed. "You must really need them. You can't just think about them, you must need them. Think about the path you took here tonight and then think about how you met me here. Then, with a bit of luck, you and the *spirit* you wish to speak with shall meet in this exact place," she continues

"So anytime we need to talk to you or Mom or Dad, we can just meet you here?"

"Well that depends...you cannot abuse this. By that I mean you will not be able to come here just to talk about boys, or complain about each other. This is serious, and you can only come for serious reasons. It is also important that you make certain no one follows you."

"Okay, so why are we here now; and since we knew nothing about this how did we get here?" Eliza asks.

With the same sweet smile Grams always gives when she is trying to make us listen to her, she says, "I guided you here. You needed to know how it is done and that I am alright. I belong here. I lived a longer life than most people ever dream of. I don't want you to be sad for me—I am not sad that I passed. You girls brought me so much joy and happiness; I do not want to bring you any pain."

"How are we supposed to do this without you Grams? You've always been there for us. You were our rock, our shoulder to cry on, and our place to turn to for advice. Now where are we supposed to go?" I argue. "I'm still just a kid, and I need you."

"And you shall always have me. That's the beauty of our heritage; I can still watch you grow up, I will still be there one day when you decide to get married, and you can still come to me for advice. I love you girls, and I will never leave you. But it is time for you to go back now. You still have a lot of work to do, I will see you soon."

Just as fast as I fell asleep, I wake up. I'm still unsure if this was just a dream, until Eliza comes running into my room. With one simple glance at each other we both know it's true. Eliza climbs into bed next to me, and we fall asleep together. Tomorrow is a new day, and as Grams said, we have lots of work to do.

◆ ◆ ◆

In the morning we wake to the sound of Matt and Luke bringing us breakfast in bed. With concerned looks on their faces, I know they are still worried about us. Eliza and I look over at each other, then look at the men we love and smile.

"Don't be so concerned boys, we're fine," Eliza insists.

As the boys walk towards us and place the breakfast trays in our laps, they both lean over and give us each a kiss.

"I'm guessing that you went on a little trip last night and saw your grandmother," Matt winks.

"You guess correctly," I reply with a giggle.

"It must have been a wonderful dream for you," he smiles.

Luke doesn't know our family secret yet, nor does he know about the Pierce family. We've kept him out of the loop so we can ensure his safety. The fewer people that know the truth about Eliza and me, not to mention the Pierce family, the better. I know how close Nathanial is to his brother Luke, and how hard it has been to keep the secret from him. I can't help but wonder if maybe it's time to tell him. Now that Grams is gone so much is going to change, and it may be better for him to know now. With mine and Eliza's powers strengthening and Grams no longer in the mortal realm, higher level *demons* will be coming for us; we are going to have to increase our training. This fight is going to be even harder than the one against the Cerberus cult.

It's hard to believe that it's been over half a year since we battled the Cerberus cult with the Pierce's and the William's, our *shape shifter* friends. So much has happened. Prior to that battle, Danika ran away and almost became Drake's, or should I say Dracula's, queen. They expected her to lead the Cerberus cult against the *vampire* leaders, the Renata, for control over all *vampires*. Thank God Caspian was there in hiding and was able to protect her and help the Pierces get her back. Poor Caspian suffered so much at the hands of Drake and his father Cyrus. They tortured him for a month to atone for helping Danika. He's still considered to be a member of the Cerberus, but he's really working undercover in order to help the Pierce family. He comes around every now and then to let us in on the plans and dealings of the Cerberus. We've all made it through the fight with the *vampires* unharmed–now it is time to fight the magickal fight. I can only hope we are just as successful.

Eliza nudges me in the side to snap me out of my thoughts. I smile and continue to eat.

While still licking her fork, Eliza says, "Thank you for breakfast. It was delicious."

"Matt and I would love to take credit for it, but Florence prepared breakfast today. I'll let her know how much you enjoyed it." Luke reaches down to take Eliza's tray. "Why don't you two get dressed and come downstairs? I think Elijah wants to go over the funeral arrangements with you. Of course, only if you're ready for that."

"Yes, of course, we'll be down soon. Thank you so much for being here for both of us." I look at Matt, remembering what happened last night, and smile.

Almost as fast as the boys leave the room, Eliza turns to me. "You didn't?"

"I didn't what?"

"Did you and Matt solidify the deal?"

"Why on earth would you ask that?" I feel the blood rushing to my cheeks as I start to blush.

"I can tell by the way you two are looking at each other. You and Matt had sex for the first time, didn't you?" She is almost busting at the seams.

"And what if we did?"

"Was it your first time, is he your first, are you his first?"

"Fine, okay, just stop with all the questions. Matt and I had sex last night. And yes, it was the first time for both of us. Are you happy now that you know my big secret?"

"Oh my God, my baby sister is now a woman. How do you feel about it today?"

"It was the right time; I needed Matt, and he needed to know that I needed him to get through all this.

We've waited a long time for this, and it couldn't have been more perfect." A huge smile breaks across my face.

She jumps across the bed, flying into my arms, squeezing me tighter than she ever has before. "I am so happy for you. I want to hear all about it."

"Not right now, you nut job. They're expecting us downstairs. Not to mention I would like to enjoy this on my own for a little while."

She flops back on her side of the bed with a pouty face, "Fine, then be that way."

With a boisterous giggle, I start to get dressed—and then I realize I have my pajamas on inside out; I must look like such a dork. I snicker as I continue to get dressed and make myself presentable before heading downstairs.

# CHARLOTTE BLACKWELL

# CHAPTER SIX
## Arrangements

The Pierce's mansion size house is the most beautiful one I've ever seen. Just a glance of the outside says royalty and old money. I can see there are several bedrooms just by looking at it from the outside. Upstairs there are several bedrooms; there must be at least a dozen overlooking the amazing grand staircase. It starts as one large staircase and then splits, leading to opposite sides of the upper level. The main foyer is gigantic, open and lined with gorgeous marble. There are several more rooms on the main floor, including a family room, formal dining room, gourmet kitchen, library, an art/music room and the games or entertainment room. Then of course there's the indoor swimming pool; we have had so many fun times in there. I like staying here–I feel safe and welcome. It's kind of funny when I think about being safe in a house full of *vampires*, but I really am.

Coming off the grand staircase from upstairs, everyone stops and stares at me. I can tell they are just worried about me, but I'm okay today. Seeing Grams last night helped put everything in perspective for me. This is just the cycle of life; we live: we die. I am just lucky; because of magick I can still see my Grams.

"Good morning everyone. We would like to thank you for all of your help, but I also want to let you know that we're okay. We've come to terms with what has happened and are ready to proceed with the arrangements in our lives without Grams." The more time I spend with the Pierces, the more formal or proper I become, because the older *vampires* are much more formal with their speech. I assume it's from being hundreds of years old. I guess just like you can't teach an old dog new tricks, you can't take away manners after many centuries. I feel very…sophisticated, that's what it is.

"That is very grown up of you Ebony, but it's okay to mourn your loss," Florence encourages.

"Thank you Florence. I really don't feel that there is anything to mourn. We've realized that Grams lived a very full life and that she passed as a happy woman."

"Well then, why don't I go over the arrangements with you?" Elijah offers.

"Thank you. Why don't we go to your office to finalize the details?"

"I will take Eliza to pick out a coffin and urn for the cremation," Florence offers.

Eliza overhears us as she comes down the stairs, "Yes Florence let's do that. I would also like to stop at the manor to pick up a few more things. Do you mind if we stay here until after the service?"

Florence walks towards Eliza, and holds both of her hands, "You two girls are like daughters to me; you can stay here as long as you like."

"Thanks; in the past year you have become like a mother to us too."

As Eliza and Florence prepare to leave for the funeral home, Elijah and I head to the office. This way everyone else can go on with their day.

◆ ◆ ◆

Elijah points to the black leather sofa in his office and takes a seat next to me, "Okay Ebony now that is just the two of us, do you want to tell me what happened?"

"How did you know I needed to talk to you?" I ask, somewhat puzzled.

"I know you well enough now to know that you would not ask to do this in private unless you have something you did not want others to hear."

"It's Luke that I am worried about." Nervously biting my lip I continue, "As you know, Luke is still in the dark about the supernatural nature of both our families. With Grams gone things are going to get more intense. I believe it's time to let Luke in on our secret."

"Why is it, after so long, you feel it is so important to tell him now?"

"Last night, I thought I was dreaming until I met Eliza in my dream. She thought she was dreaming too, then Grams came to us." I continue to explain the events of last night to Elijah, "This is why we are so at peace today."

"That definitely explains a lot. I must say that I am delighted to know that you truly have not lost your grandmother. It is also wonderful that you will get to know your mother and father after so many years."

"Yes, they told us they would return to help us train for our fight against Naberius. It sounds as though this may be a bigger fight than the one in which we helped you fight the Cerberus."

"I think we made a great team against an evil *vampire* cult, and I think we can do even better against evil *demons*. We are all much stronger now. Always remember, our family is ready to fight, right beside you, as you did for us." Elijah puts his arm over my shoulder, "Now, we need to finalize the funeral arrangements. After that, we will concentrate on the fight ahead."

In agreement, we begin to go over the final arrangements. Elijah has everything taken care of and only needs us to accept what he has planned.

"Ebony, I also want you to know that Florence and I will take care of all the financial aspects of the funeral. You girls don't need to worry yourselves about money now or ever. Your grandmother took care of us when we needed it, and we will be here for you now. Your grandmother wouldn't have it any other way."

Reviewing the details for the funeral, I agree to everything Elijah has planned. This is going to be a beautiful service and will do Grams justice.

"It appears that you have done a wonderful job. I think Grams would appreciate the service you have put together as much as I do. Thank you." Small tears trickle down my face before I wipe them away. "I especially like that you are arranging a small gathering at the manor after the town service. That is where she would've wanted it."

"It is my belief that your Grams would have wanted a death ritual or the requiem. She always told me that death is celebrated and honored, not feared. Death is simply a part of the cycle of life."

Surprised by Elijah's knowledge of *witches* and our beliefs I add, "Yes I believe she would too. From what I have read in the *Book of Shadows* the requiem can include the deceased person being buried with their ritual tools. Items such as their wand, athame, etc.; some choose to be buried in their ceremonial robes. Many *witches* believe in reincarnation, and most believe in a 'Summerland' where the soul can rest between lives."

"Is Summerland where you saw your Grams last night?" Elijah asks with interest.

"I don't believe so. I think that is a sacred place only *spirits* can travel to. I also know that some of us believe that the dead become *ancestor spirits*, and protect and guide us from the spirit world. This is similar to what Grams was explaining. I believe that my family is following that path. It has also been implied that all of these things are possible, and that it is up to the soul how they choose to spend their afterlife."

"Thank you for sharing this with me Ebony. I very much enjoy learning about your family and the belief system you have."

"It helps me to explain to others; unfortunately, I'm not really allowed to tell other people I know this kind of stuff."

"Always know that my family and I are here for you, no matter what. You can always teach us what you are learning. After so many years, it can be difficult to find new things to learn."

"Well here is another fact that you may not know. Some pagan traditions are very focused on the dead; on honoring the ancestors, giving them offerings, keeping their memories alive. Samhain or Halloween is all about the dead–it is primarily an ancestor holiday. It is a time to honor, and even communicate with, those loved ones who have passed, and also a time to say good bye to those who died in the past year."

"Interesting; and what is it that you believe, Ebony?

"After meeting with Grams last night, I believe those whom we love become our ancestor spirits when they die. They continue to love us as they did in life, and they guide, protect, and aid us in subtle ways. They can even communicate with us in dreams, meditation and through divination techniques such as scrying…similar to how we tried to locate Danika when she ran away. After a period of time, they may choose to be reborn–to reincarnate. It is kinda a milkshake of most beliefs," I joke.

"Well just remember, death is not an ending–it is just part of the cycle, part of the wheel that *vampires* rarely complete. You can consider your Grams lucky to have completed her wheel," Elijah says with a hint of despair, knowing that he never will.

# CHAPTER SEVEN
## Remembering

The next few days pass quickly and before we know it's time for Grams' funeral. With the service about to start Eliza and I enter the funeral home and take our seats up front. Matt and Luke are already sitting there waiting for us. The Pierce family sits one row back, as it is a small funeral home with very little seating room. Staring straight ahead at the beautiful mahogany casket, I try to remember how peaceful Grams was the night she came to us. The picture of Grams, right behind her casket, is fairly recent, showing her beautiful silver hair. On either side are smaller pictures of Grams, one with Mom and Dad and another one with Eliza and myself. Beautiful bouquets cover almost the entire altar, the largest one filled with lilies, Grams favorite flower.

The funeral director rises to the podium, "I would like to welcome everyone here to celebrate the life of Ms. Edwina Triggs. Edwina was born, raised and lived out her life here in Wenham, Massachusetts. She was an active and productive member of our community, and she will be missed by all who knew her. With the passing of her daughter and son-in-law, Edwina took on the challenge of raising her two infant granddaughters into wonderful young women. Edwina was the type of citizen that was always willing to help others, in any way that she could. Whether it was serving Christmas dinner at the homeless shelter, sorting out care packages for those in need, or volunteering her time at the crisis center. Our town always knew we could count on her."

I look around the funeral home not expecting many people to be here, but the place is full; wall-to-wall and out the door. I always knew Grams was amazing, I just never knew that everyone else knew it too.

The service lasts about forty-five minutes and the director paints Grams in a perfect light. He does a beautiful job, as did Florence and Elijah in the planning. Following the recession line Eliza, myself, and those closest to us will go to the crematory. Following will be time for our private service at the manor.

"I'm glad the formal part is over. But it was beautiful," Eliza admits.

I agree. "It was perfect. I can't believe the turn out. Who knew that so many people in town cared about Grams?"

"Ms. Edwina was one of the most amazing people I have met in all my centuries." Florence hugs my sister and me.

"How are you two holding up?" Matt asks.

Taking hold of his hand, I confess, "I think we're doing okay, really. I am just anxious to get the cremation over with and get back to the manor."

"Well then, we should proceed to the crematorium," Elijah recommends.

♦ ♦ ♦

"Would you like to go to the viewing area for the cremation, or the private family room?" asks the tall lanky attendant.

"Girls, what would you prefer? Either option is fine," Constance asks.

Eliza answers, "I would like to go to the viewing room; what about you Ebony?"

"Um, yeah, I guess I'll come." I wonder if I'm ready to watch Gram's body being pushed into an open fire. I know that it is only her physical body and not her soul, but the visual image might be a bit much for me to take.

"Are you girls alright to do that on your own, or would you prefer someone to come with you?" Constance inquires.

"No way, you are all family. I…we'd like to have you all come with us. Of course, if you are alright with that," I declare.

"You're asking if we're alright about joining you during the cremation. I'm certain that we can handle it. What about you boys?" Isaac asks Nathanial, Matt, and Luke.

"We'll do whatever our girls want us to do," claims Luke.

"Thank you. I guess it has been decided–we'll go and watch from the viewing room," Eliza announces solemnly to the attendant.

"Yes ma'am, if you and your family would please follow me. It is just upstairs."

Our group of thirteen enters a room with a large glass wall, and as we look through we can see below us a conveyer belt at least eight feet long. A large cast iron furnace-type machine meets the end of the conveyer belt.

My thoughts turn briefly to Caspian, who couldn't make it to the service as he is being watched too closely by the leaders of the Cerberus, and still hasn't taken back his day crystal. Ever since he accidently killed his girlfriend Ashley, he has committed himself to the darkness. Recently he was reunited with his *vampire* family the Pierces, but he remains undercover with the *vampire* cult that we battled early in the year. It's nice to have someone on the inside watching over things for us. When I look out the glass window and bring my thoughts back to where we are, it becomes a little more than I can handle.

The tears begin to well up in my eyes, "This is not quite what I expected."

"Are you okay, Ebony?" Sophia puts her arm around me.

Flames shoot out of the heavy iron opened door. To me it looks like the large gaping mouth of hell ready to swallow Grams. With a gasp, I reply,"Oh lord, I hope so." The tears that have been building from deep within me begin to sting my eyes even more.

We all watch as Grams' casket is wheeled in and placed on the conveyer. Trying to choke back the tears, I sniff, and the tears begin to flow freely out of me, running down my cheeks. Just as fast as the tears fall I wipe them away and turn to bury my head into Sophia's shoulder.

"Ebony, do you want to leave? Matt and I will come with you," she consoles.

"No, I wanna stay. It's just emotional."

I look at Eliza who is standing strong as a rock, and I wonder why I am unable to be that strong.

Grams casket starts to move down the conveyer belt and enters the fierce fire of orange and red flames with a hint of blue at the hot spots. I can hear the instant crackling of the mahogany coffin through the thick glass wall. Everyone in the room is deathly quiet. I can almost hear the five beating hearts begin to pound faster. We watch as the entire casket is devoured by the oven and flames, which begin to burn large, and the crackling is unbearable. Below us they close the same iron door they opened just minutes ago. The heaviness of the door makes a loud bang like a gunshot. Moments later the attendant enters the viewing room.

"Can I offer anyone some water? I know how traumatizing this can be."

"Thank you, that would be appreciated," Florence answers.

He goes to the fridge at the back of the room and removes enough water bottles for all of us. "The process of cremation takes about two hours, and then another hour before the remains are ready for you to take. You are more than welcome to wait here. Another option, if it is preferable to you, is for us to deliver the remains to the location of your choice."

"I think it is best to get you girls back to the manor and a little something to eat," Florence recommends.

Eliza puts her hand on my shoulder, "I agree with Florence. Come on Ebony. Let's go home. Grams wouldn't want us to suffer like this."

Matt and Sophia help lead me out of the crematorium. Seeing Grams body being burned that way affected me more than anything I've ever experienced before. I feel weak and nauseated, unsure if I will make it back down the stairs. Matt tightens his grip around my waist for support. With him by my side I already begin to feel my strength returning.

# CHAPTER EIGHT
## Confessions

Arriving back at the manor I feel a slight release of tension. We need to set up for the requiem. Eliza, Sophia, and Nathanial decide it is time to let Luke in on our secrets. Without knowing our family history, he'll be very confused about what's about to happen. We go to the same family room where Sophia, Nathanial, Matt and I had the same discussion earlier this year. We all hope that he will handle it as well as Matt and Nathanial both did.

Eliza takes a deep breath and with a shaky voice she begins. "Well Luke, we have known one another for a while now, and have been together for over six months. You've been here for me through one of the most difficult times in my life. I think it is time for you to know everything about me. I hate to admit this, but I have been keeping a secret from you, and hope that you will understand why I didn't tell you sooner."

"Should we go upstairs so that we can talk in private?"

"No, everyone here is prepared to help me explain."

"So they all know what you have been keeping from me?" he asks with a glance to his little brother Nathanial.

"Yes Bro, I know. Just understand this was not for me to share with you. Eliza needed to do this on her own terms."

"Okay, I'm all ears. I hope that everything is alright.'

"Well, I guess the best way is just come out and say it. I'll be happy to answer any questions you have." With a huge sigh, "My sister and I are *witches*. We are real life, magick practicing, powerful *witches*. We come from a long line of some of the most powerful *witches* in the world. Our ancestors date back to Salem, before the *witch* trials took place. We only found out last year, when Ebony turned sixteen. We started to gain supernatural powers, and then Grams taught us the old ways. Since that time we've been working hard to help make this a better place. We fight *demons* and banish them deep into the underworld so that they can never return. The day Grams died, we banished a *demon* right here in the kitchen."

We all watch Luke closely for his reaction, but he's blank faced, void of emotion. Then he cracks a smile, "You're telling me that you are descendents of Salem *witches*? With how interested I am on the history of this town and the supernatural forces that surround it, you didn't think you could trust me with this information?"

"It wasn't that I can't or don't trust you. It was that…well I was scared of how you would react. Having an interest in something and knowing that it is real is completely different."

"And Nate, how long have you known this?" He turns to his brother.

"I found out around Christmas time last year," Nathanial answers.

"So you felt that you could trust everyone in this room, including my brother, more than me. I can't believe you told my brother, before I even knew you."

"The sisters did not tell Nate, I did." Sophia confesses.

"And what gave you the right to share Ebony's and Eliza's secret with him? If they share something like that with you, my little brother being your boyfriend does not automatically give you permission to spill everyone's secrets. Now on the same note; as my brother, Nate, you should have told me." Luke starts getting upset.

"Well, see, my family has a secret of our own. And in telling him my secret, their secret eventually came out," Sophia defends.

"So you guys are *witches* too?" Luke assumes.

"No, we too have supernatural powers, but we are not *witches*. My family and I are *vampires*."

"You're what?" Luke is startled. "And you aren't concerned about this Nate?"

"Not at all—the Pierce family has everything under control. They do not attack, kill, or feed off of mortals." Nate smiles and holds Sophia's hand.

"Okay, this is a lot to process. Nate, you said you found out around Christmas; when exactly did you find out?"

"Do you remember when you first met Sophia and had pulled out your history books?"

"Yeah, now that you mention it I do. There is a picture of the family at a witch-hunt in the area. You thought that looked like Sophia in the picture." The expression on his face proves that he is putting two and two together.

"It was me and my family. That picture is the day that we found Matilda; and that is the night that I admitted what I was to Nathanial," Sophia confirms.

Luke sits in shock that his brother has accepted a *vampire* to love. "How do you know you can trust them?" Luke questions.

"The night of winter formal, when I was attacked, the Pierce family saved my life. A rogue vampire tried to kill me. Alexander destroyed my attacker, and Sophia healed me. If it wasn't for them, I'd be dead."

Luke sits back in his chair, attempting to process all the information he is getting. The silence is overwhelming for the second time today.

Luke stands up from his chair, walks over to Eliza, and kisses her on the forehead. "This is all a little shocking. The only thing I can really say is, Eliza Triggs, I love you and accept you for who you are. Sophia, you and your family have been amazing to my family, and if my brother can trust you, so can I."

The tension in the room dissipates as we all breathe a sigh of relief.

"I would love to hear more and learn more, but today is not the day. Today is about Ms. Edwina and honoring her. You can tell me more about your supernatural lives later. Thank you for finally having the confidence to tell me," Luke says with dignity.

CHARLOTTE BLACKWELL

# CHAPTER NINE
## Summerland

The doorbell rings and Danika, the newest member of the Pierce family, rises to see who's there. Constance found Danika about two years ago, outside of the hospital she worked at in Canada. Constance knew the Embrace had already begun and the young girl had been left by her maker. The Pierce family welcomed her and began to train her to assimilate amongst us mortals. That is when they moved back to Wenham in hopes of getting her a blessed day crystal like theirs. I know Danika still feels sometimes like she doesn't belong. She's had her share of tough times since becoming a vampire, but should feel lucky to have a family like the Pierces. They've been there for her and helped her through her Embrace and the mistakes she has made since that day. Danika, just like any other teenager, rebelled not long ago, easily influenced by Drake. Drake is the new leader of the Cerberus and wanted her for his queen. He lured her, the same way drug dealers lure teens, with the promise of feeling better on fresh blood. Caspian was able to help rescue her from the underground *vampire* club Drake was holding her in. Sophia and Danika have never seen eye to eye, although Sophia has been trying hard to make things work. She doesn't want to push Danika away again.

A few moments later Danika re-enters the family room, holding Grams urn. She looks around the room. "It was the crematorium; where should I put Ms. Edwina's ashes?"

Florence gets up and takes the urn; she takes it to the kitchen and places it on the apothecary cabinet.

"Okay girls, I think it is time that we prepare for your grandmas ritual," Florence adds as she comes back into the family room. "What do you need us to do?"

Ebony opens the *Book of Shadows* to the requiem ritual. "We need to gather white candles, a white altar cloth, and white flowers."

"I thought white was for weddings?" Luke asks.

"White is the color of death and mourning in many countries," Elijah points out.

"As a *witch* we believe it is also a reminder of rebirth. During this ritual we will focus on that," Eliza adds.

"It all sounds very interesting; I can't wait to learn more. Thank you for deciding to share this with me. Now, what else do you need me to go and get for you?" Luke gives her a hug.

"Okay, we need a picture of Grams. There is a nice one right there on the fireplace mantel. Also a vase full of flowers, with enough for all of us, which you can find on the kitchen table."

Luke begins to gather the items from around the house as the rest of us began to clean. In order for us to perform any ritual, we have to cleanse the area before we cast a circle. We go about sweeping and dusting the area all in a clockwise motion. I take a dried sage wrap, light it and cleanse the area by brushing the smoke around. I can hear Eliza calling out items to Luke, along with the thumping of his large size thirteen feet running across the hardwood floors.

"Next we need a pitcher of water and a basin, to be set up just outside the circle for ritual hand-washing." Eliza then takes the urn with Grams ashes and places it on the altar.

Our beautiful, handmade alter has the triquetra on the front door which opens to reveal a storage area for our ritual items. On the top, two triquetra symbols with small circles carved into the center makes the perfect place for candles. The triquetra is a special symbol to our family and a symbol of our magick. I've always wondered who made this alter; today it is an extra special part of our ritual.

"We need to fill the cauldron with earth, and a bowl with seeds. The seeds can be found in the apothecary cabinet, and the cauldron should be under the counter," she announces.

"I have to ask, what is all this for?" Nathanial questions with a puzzled look upon his face.

"This is so each person can plant a seed in the cauldron which will symbolize new life," Eliza explains. "Remember, this is just as new for us as it is you. We have never done a death ritual before so we are learning just like you. The basic elements of the ritual will remain the same though."

It appears that everything is ready and in place. With a brief explanation about rituals and circles to those amongst us, we begin. I allow the others to cleanse with the bowl of water and I go last. Once everyone has taken their seat, we all begin to relax with three cleansing breaths in and out. With small, paced steps, I walk the room lighting the candles. Matilda remembers the incense and it is placed on the alter; I light the small cone allowing the smoky scent to fill the room. I cast the circle, and invite the deities, God and Goddess and loved ones to join us.

Eliza stands in front of the alter, "We are all here to remember Edwina Triggs, born January sixth, 1925, and died August second, 2011. She has gone on to Summerland and now awaits rebirth."

We encourage our friends to meditate on one's own personal experiences with death, or on a last communication with our loved one, or even on a remembrance of past lives. I pass around the photo, which is kept in a beautiful white frame; each person looks at it, holds it before them so that it's facing the rest of the group, and relates a favored anecdote about Grams. I begin to tear up again at all the wonderful things being said about her. The amazing part is, I agree with every statement.

Eliza has a final word before the circle is opened. With everyone holding hands, she speaks to the Goddess. She speaks about the turning of the wheel of rebirth for Grams who is now gone, and how we will all meet her again. Once again, she makes note of Grams many wonderful qualities.

"In remembrance I would like everyone to have a flower to take home as a farewell gift. This will help us in remembering her."

We lower our heads in a moment of silence. I slowly lift my eyes to see three faint white figures. It doesn't take me long to realize Mom, Dad and Grams are all here to join us. Before commencing the ritual we all enjoy cakes and ale, which is really just a fancy word for cookies and juice. This helps to ground us from the transfer of energy involved in rituals. I then open the circle. As the circle opens, everyone exchanges hugs and a wonderful peaceful feeling overcomes us all. We all watch in amazement as the three white figure rise to the ceiling and disappear into thousands of tiny white flecks resembling snowflakes, right before our eyes.

"Thank you to each and every one of you for sharing in this ritual with us. It means so much to have those we love around us. What started as a difficult and somber situation has turned into a peaceful celebration of life," Eliza shares.

Isaac puts his arms around us, as Constance passes out glasses of champagne to celebrate the wonderful life Grams had. He raises his glass in a toast, "We are so glad that we are able to be here and show our support for you girls and your Grams. If not for her and her mother, we would not be able to exist the way we do. Your ancestors pulled us out of the night and the shadows; they returned us to the light. The Triggs women have helped us to become civilized members of society. For that we are forever indebted to you. We will ensure we are available to every generation, as long as we walk the earth. Here is to the Triggs women."

# CHAPTER TEN
## Surprise

Things haven't been that different since Grams passed, I can't believe it's been three weeks already. School starts again in just a few days and I'm totally unprepared. I really miss Grams, when it comes to stuff like this; she was great at keeping me organized. The whole gang is getting ready to go and do some serious shopping. Sophia, Alexander, Matilda, and Danika will meet us at the mall. Nathanial is picking up Matt and they should be here any minute to pick me up. Eliza is happy to have the day alone with Luke since he leaves to go back to college tomorrow.

"Kay, Eliza, they're here. We're all spending the night at the Pierce's again so you and Luke have the night to yourselves," I shout to her from down the hall.

She quickly comes down the hall towards the door. "Have fun kids. Call me if you need me."

She waits at the door; as I get to Nathanial's car Luke jumps out to join her. I can't help but grind my teeth every time she calls me kid—really, I mean she's

75

only a few years older than me. Taking a deep breath to calm my nerves I close the car door and they both wave us off. We watch as they already start kissing on the porch, and with a chuckle we leave.

◆ ◆ ◆

Once we all meet up the boys go their own way and the girls head for the clothing stores. It's been a very crazy summer, and we just need some typical girl time to catch up. It's so nice to have meaningless little chitchat with the girls. Danika is even starting to fit in a little better now that all the other concerns have been straightened out and taken care of. I have come to realize that she is a smart kid. I sometimes wonder, how could she have been so stupid to be fooled by a bunch of underground, violent, bloodsucking *vampires*? I'm hoping today that all four of us girls can just open up a little bit and share a little bit of ourselves with each other. I still haven't told Sophia about mine and Matt's relationship reaching the next level. I'm also hoping she'll soon open up a little bit more about Caspian. It's nice that he comes around every now and then, but I know that she hopes he will rejoin their family for good.

"So Ebony, how have you been doing? We really haven't had much time to just talk with all the crap going on this summer," Sophia makes note.

"I know; I miss our girl chats and slumber parties. I'm doing okay. It really helps to be buried in our lessons, and preparing for what may come."

"Well, you know I'm always willing to help with a good *witch* project," Sophia smiles.

Matilda gives Sophia a little nudge, "We're all here to help. Right Danika?"

In her sweet, insecure voice Danika replies. "Of course Ebony; that is, if you want me to help after all I put you guys through?"

Sophia stops cold, turns to Danika and insists, "I'm going to say this one last time Danika. You are still new to our life–I'm still cautious about you and with good reason. Now with that said, you made a mistake–you were fooled. Many teenagers experience the same thing. You're a *vampire* now and can't allow yourself to fall in to the same trap as other kids your age. That's why we're here, to help you and protect you. You need to learn to trust us, just as we need to learn to trust you."

I can see Danika getting emotional, and I pull her off to the side away from the others. "Danika, you can't keep beating yourself up over it. We've all forgiven you. You can also look at it that you helped to bring Caspian back, even if just a little, into the lives of your family. We all love you, and yes, I would love your help with my studies. So let's try to forget about the past because everyone makes mistakes. Okay?"

"Thank you Ebony." She opens up and gives me a hug.

"Okay, now back to shopping. This is supposed to be fun," Matilda jokes as she drags us back to the group.

"Well everyone is staying at our place tonight, so girl time it is!" Sophia smiles and runs off to the next store.

"Good, I have something I need to tell you," I admit.

We continue on like typical girls for a few hours, then with bags in hand we meet the boys for a quick bite to eat for those of us that need it.

♦ ♦ ♦

Shortly after, we head back to the Pierce house and prepare for an old style slumber party. Now at home, our *vampire* friends can gather for one of Florence's gourmet blood meals. Sophia has explained to me that Florence is very good at preparing blood to resemble mortal meals. She infuses the donated blood bags with such things as citrus or herbs and makes soups, and blood pudding, even fancy ice cream. She even insists that they all sit together and eat like a family. She does her best to make their existence as close as she can to mortality. Isaac is a hematologist and has been working for years to create a synthetic blood using various expired blood products and such. It has been a passion of his ever since he lost a young patient to a rare blood disease. I heard that Isaac is getting closer to perfecting his synthetic blood and they are using less and less human and animal blood. Nathanial, Matt and I all visit in the family room as our friends enjoy their meal.

♦ ♦ ♦

After the Pierce's finish their dinner, we start getting ready for a night of movies. Everyone grabs some pillows and blankets to get comfy on the floor. The boys go to pick a movie from a large selection stored in the library as Matilda and Danika go to make some popcorn for us. Sophia and I get some drinks. The day crystals they wear give them the ability to drink and eat mortal food without getting ill like most *vampires* would, although they usually only eat for show as it doesn't sustain them. Florence has prepared some pink lemonade for us mortals, and what Sophia calls a lovely blood punch for the *vampires*. We're definitely an eclectic group of friends, mortals, a future *guardian, vampires* and *witches*. All we need is the *shape shifters* to join in on the fun. We met them when we were preparing for the battle with the Cerberus; they are ancestors of the land and have sworn to protect those that inhabit it now. Lucky for us, we have become very good friends with them since.

"Hey, has anyone talked to Tamo lately?" I ask.

"Alex was out there just the other day. They are all doing well and apologize for not making the funeral," Sophia remembers.

"I will have to give Dakota a call or maybe a text soon, and see how the pack is doing."

The smell of popcorn wafts into the room and overpowers me. Jumping to my feet, I run to the washroom. I'm certain even without the Pierce's super hearing the entire house could hear me puking like a mad man.

"Ebony, you okay? I brought you some water." Sophia knocks at the door.

"Come on in."

She enters with the glass of water that I quickly chug.

"I don't know what came over me. The smell of the popcorn is just making me so ill."

"Here, let me see if I can help. Maybe you had something bad to eat at the mall. I know it does it to me every time," she jokes.

"Ha-ha, you should become a comedian. Please try something. I feel another wave coming on."

"Okay lay down on the floor mat there," she instructs.

As I lay down, Sophia gently places her hands on my stomach, and begins to focus. In just moments I begin to feel better and she stops.

"Thanks Sophia, I feel much better."

"Well I hate to tell you, but it won't last for long," she says with a very surprised tone.

"Really, I must have got a real bad batch. I think I'll avoid sushi for a bit."

"Ebony, it wasn't the sushi."

"What was it? Am I going to be okay? You look really concerned."

"You'll be fine, don't worry. So what was it you wanted to tell me earlier? I think maybe now is a good time since we're alone," she begins to pry.

"Well I might as well just tell you. Matt and I finally took the next step; I'm now a woman, so to speak," I admit with a goofy grin.

"A woman, more than you know. That is totally what I thought you were going to say. So when did this happen? I want all the juicy details."

"Actually, it was the night Grams passed. It happened here. We didn't plan it, but it was amazing."

"I'm so happy for you, but I just want to be the responsible one and make sure that you and Matt use protection."

"Well that first time, no we didn't–it happened so unexpectedly we didn't have any. But of course now we do. I figure it was okay, since we were both virgins and it was only one time." I blush a little at the admission.

"Ebony, you should know better than that." She starts to lecture, "I'm sorry, I don't mean to nag you. I just worry about you and Matt."

"Thanks, but really there is nothing to worry about. We always are safe now," I defend. "Oh no, here it comes again." I lean in to the toilet.

"Ebony, I'll be right back, I'm going to get Constance to help," she mentions with concern as she leaves the washroom.

Within minutes I hear a knock on the door, "Ebony, may I come in? Sophia said you aren't feeling well," Constance requests.

"Yeah."

Constance and Sophia enter and close the door behind them. Constance places a cool cloth on my forehead.

"Here sweetie, this may help." Constance hands me a small cup of medicine.

"What's this?" I ask.

"It will help you feel better," she replies.

Sophia gently rubs my back, "So Ebony, I told Constance what was going on. I also mentioned that I attempted to heal you and what I sensed."

"It is bad, I knew it. What's wrong with me?"

"Well sweetie," Constance wipes the tears from my eyes. "It is nothing that will kill you."

With a slight hint of panic I take a deep breath. "Okay, well that's good. So then what is wrong?"

"It appears as though you are pregnant," Constance shares.

"I could sense it when I was trying to heal your suspected food poisoning. That appears to be morning sickness," Sophia confesses.

I sit back on the floor and begin to panic, breathing faster and faster. "You're freaking kidding right–this is just to make sure that Matt and I use protection from now on, right?" The tears stream down my face.

"Oh honey, I wish it was. Are you okay? We will all be here to help you," Sophia cradles me in her arms as I sob.

"What am I going to tell Matt? Oh my God, school is starting in a few days; great way to start senior year."

"We have time to figure this all out; let's just make sure. I will book you for an early ultrasound. Technically you should not even know yet. I even find it weird that you are feeling the symptoms so early," Constance informs me.

"We need to get you calmed down and back out there before everyone else wonders what is going on," Sophia recommends.

Knowing they are both right, I try to calm down. I clean myself up and rejoin everyone for a night of movies and games. I need to do my best to keep up a façade that everything is normal, at least until Constance can do the ultra sound tomorrow. After I know for sure, I will find a way to tell Matt. The panic begins to take over again as I wonder how he'll react–how everyone will react, and what will happen at school. I just don't know if I can handle this–I'm not even seventeen yet. At this very moment I am glad Grams is not here to witness this. I start to freak a little more remembering that Grams and my parents probably already know. What they must think of me. I know that I am going to be letting everyone down. It was our first time; it was supposed to be special. I mean, it was special, but a baby…Oh God!

# CHARLOTTE BLACKWELL

# CHAPTER ELEVEN
## Confirmation

As soon as we wake up, Constance informs the others that she needs Sophia and me to help with something. We easily sneak off to the hospital, where she can perform the ultra sound. Once there Constance leads us into her office for privacy.

She sees a nurse friend and asks, "Kathi, can you please get the portable ultra sound for me, and bring it to my office? Please use the utmost discretion."

"Of course Dr. Pierce, I will only be a moment. Do you require anything else?" the nurse asks. She seems kind hearted, a little older, maybe fifty or so. She has short strawberry blond hair and tiny teal eyes, which appear to be permanently smiling. Her rosy cheeks just add to the softness of her demeanor.

"No that will be all, thank you Kathi," she says and shuts the door.

As we wait, I hope that Sophia has made a mistake. The only problem is that in a year I have yet to see her be wrong. She's been working on Mrs. McCord,

Nathanial's mom, of course without her knowing. The McCords have wanted another child since Nathanial was born. Unfortunately, Mrs. McCord sustained internal damage during childbirth and has not been able to conceive again. Since Sophia can't tell them about her and her powers, she is healing Nathanial's mom without her knowledge. That's why it is taking so long; she has to do the healing in small increments. Yet here I am not wanting a baby, and preparing to confirm that I will be a mother before graduation.

"I was just thinking about Mrs. McCord; how's the healing going for her?" I ask.

Sophia smiles, "I think I have almost repaired all her internal damage. Nate and I talked to them, just to make sure they would still want to have another child. I mean Nate and Luke are both men now, they are almost done raising children."

"I assume they still do?"

"I have never seen anyone light up at the thought of a baby the way those two did. Nate's mom said she would never give up the opportunity to love someone. They have even considered adoption or fostering a child." Sophia looks at me and realizes what she just said. "I am so sorry Ebony, I didn't mean…"

The tears start to come again, "I know, and I understand. How can I be so upset over something so wonderful, that so many others would love to have?"

There is a knock on the door, and my heart almost jumps out of my chest. Nurse Kathi walks in with this rather large machine on wheels. She places it next to the sofa in Constance's office.

"Don't worry Ebony; it is not as scary as it looks. Come lie down on the sofa and lift your shirt up a little. I am going to put a little of this blue gel on your stomach—it can feel a little cold." Constance warns. "Then I am going to use this little handle, and just by moving it around on the gel, we will get a picture of your internal organs. You can watch everything on this little screen. I will describe it as we go."

"Okay, I think I'm ready." I squeeze Sophia's hand.

"Oh my, it's a good thing I am a *vampire* otherwise this would really hurt," Sophia tries to lighten the mood.

"Okay Ebony, here comes the gel. Remember to breathe—it is going to be okay."

I jump a little when the gel plops on my stomach and Constance spreads it around. I try to watch the screen but can't make anything out.

"See this here, this is your uterus," Constance explains the shadow on the screen. "The uterus is normally not quite this visible."

"So what does that mean?" I question.

"Well, do you see this little dot on the side of the uterus?"

"Yeah, what is that?"

"That is the embryo—Ebony, you're pregnant."

"And that is my baby?"

"Yeah, sweetie. That will be yours and Matt's baby."

Sophia starts to rub my hand, "Are you okay Ebony?'

I keep my eyes on the screen and nod my head, feeling calm; the same way Matt makes me feel. "Yeah, I really am. Can you believe Matt and I created that the first time we were ever together? It's a miracle, like it's meant to be. My baby was created through love. Even the fact that this happened the day of Gram's passing should mean something."

"I must say I am surprised at your reaction," Sophia says with slight concern.

"Oh don't get me wrong, I'm terrified. I'm so not ready for this, and like the kids at school don't tease me enough. I have no idea what I'm going to do. How will I ever go to college with a baby?" I start to panic again as reality sets in. I'm only sixteen, still just a kid myself, and have not even started senior year yet. I'm going to be a mommy. What the hell were we thinking not using protection? I begin to feel really hot and dizzy; it's hard to breath. Suddenly everything goes black.

♦ ♦ ♦

I wake up on the floor of a cave; I recognize it as the same cave where I saw Grams that first night. Slowly, I get up to my feet and proceed down the same hall, wondering what I'm doing here. The last thing I remember, I was in Constance's office; oh God, I'm pregnant! I need Grams, that must be why am here. Then I see it in front of me, the white light, and I know she is coming. I can feel the white light surrounding me. The warmth coming from it is wrapping me in an embrace as if she is hugging me, and peace enters my soul.

"Grams is that you? I need you so bad right now. I have made a terrible mess of things and I don't know how to fix it."

"We are all here for you, Ebony. Your mother, father and I are all here. We know what's going on and one lesson that you need to learn is anything can happen. Don't ever think that can't happen to you. I know both you and Matt are smart kids, therefore the two of you should've known better. Now that my mini lecture is out of the way, we also want you to know that your life isn't over. Things are going to be...well, difficult; I'm not going to lie to you. I know you're a fighter. For crying out loud, you take on demons on a regular basis, I think you can handle a few soiled diapers and sleepless nights."

"Ebony just because your father and I have not been physically there for you doesn't mean that we've not been with you. We have seen you and Matt grow together as a couple and know the two of you can make it through this. You'll be seventeen next month; that's only one year younger than I was when I had your sister. I just hope that you have a better chance at being a mother then I did," my mother admits.

Just as quickly as I arrived, it all fades and I feel a pull back to my physical body.

♦ ♦ ♦

"Ebony, Ebony are you okay? Open your eyes and look at me," Sophia's voice gets louder.

I open my eyes and realize I am back in Constance's office. Sophia's in a panic, shaking me and trying to wake me. I have never seen her like this before.

I'm sure this is about as close to terrified as *vampires* can get.

With a huge sigh, "Ebony I'm so glad you're okay. I've never sensed anything like that before, what the hell happened?" Sophia hugs me so tight, I can barely breathe.

"I'm okay. I didn't realize I needed my Grams, and without knowing it inadvertently went to see her. My mother and father were there too. They all know that I'm pregnant, but they all have so much confidence in me."

I turn back and look at a little spot still frozen on the screen from the exam. In less than a year that will be my baby. I feel better now. I know I should've been more careful. But what's done is done, and it's time to move on and make this right.

# CHAPTER TWELVE
## Surprising Turn

Driving back to the Pierce house, I try to decide how I'm going to tell Matt. I think it is best to tell him today; this isn't something I should keep from him. Doing it at the Pierce house will be the best; being surrounded by those that we love and that won't judge either of us will help to make it easier. Pulling up the drive my nerves begin to get the best of me. My heart starts to race and the stickiness of sweat on my palms confirms it all. I try to remember what Grams and Mom said to me. They're right, Matt and I will get through this together. I always knew one day Matt and I would have a family. I just didn't expect it to be so soon.

"You're back already?" Alexander notes, while looking at his watch.

"Yeah it didn't take long," Sophia answers. The two siblings slowly walk into the other room, knowing fully that they need to remain close by, but still giving us some privacy. Alexander is fully aware of the situation, courtesy of his telepathy. Sometimes it is annoying not having any privacy from him, but most of the time it's helpful.

Somewhat worried, I walk inside and see Matt. I give him a hug and a tear falls down my cheek.

"What's the matter beautiful, did something happen?" Wiping the tears from my face he places his hands on either of my shoulders, with concern on his face.

"Well, I went to the hospital with Constance so she could run some tests on me, and find out why I was so ill last night," I begin to admit.

"What is it, are you okay? Are you sick?" He leads me towards a chair.

"Well, no I am not sick. Although there is something going on that we need to talk about." Without realizing that I'm holding my breath, my lungs start to burn. With a huge intake of air, the pain subsides.

"Okay, you can tell me anything. I'll always be here for you. I just hope you're going to be okay."

"I will be, but Matt, you and I…" I start to stutter.

"You're not breaking up with me, are you?" He sits back, with the worry in his brow growing.

"NO, never, but um," I can feel my heart pounding through my chest again. "See the night we…ah…um, first made love…well, we were a little caught up in the moment."

"Yeah, we can't be that careless again," he smiles.

"Well, it doesn't really matter anymore, because I'm pregnant." I start to cry again.

Matt's face goes blank as the color drains from his face. He lowers his head into his hands, takes a deep breath and looks at me. Noticing the tears streaming down my face in full force, with my knees pulled to my chest in the fetal position, he kneels in front of me and holds me.

"I am so sorry Ebony, I'm just surprised."

"I know, I was too. What are we going to do?"

Matt stands and says, "I'm just going to get some water, would you like some? Then we can figure things out."

He hurries out of the room, and I don't know what to do with myself. Is this it, will he run? Will he even come back? Sophia comes and gets me; she leads me into the family room where the entire Pierce family is. Florence quickly runs to me and holds me in her motherly fashion.

"Ebony, I understand how difficult this must be for you, but we are here for you as always. I have told you that you are like another daughter to me, and your baby will also be a part of this family." She softly kisses my forehead.

Matt comes back in with two bottles of water and hands me one, then sits next to me and holds my hand. "I am glad that you're all here. This is a pretty shocking time for us, and I'm glad that we've got friends like you to help us through it."

"Matt, I must say you are extremely calm," Elijah observes.

"I guess I am. I have a slight admission to make. The Great Ones came to me a while ago and forewarned me that something would happen that could change our lives. They never told me that I was going to be a father;

just that it was something to solidify mine and Ebony's relationship. So with this information I decided to prepare for what was to come."

"What do you mean by prepare?" I ask, "How on earth could you be prepared for having a baby at seventeen?" I don't mean to be rude, but am concerned that I might be coming off that way.

"Well, I wrote a letter to you." He handed me a folded paper, "I needed to write down how I feel about you, in case when the time came I wasn't able to get the words out."

Matt pulls me up to stand with him, in front of the ones we care most about. "You and I have been inseparable since the day I moved to Wenham. In just a few days we begin our final year of high school. After that we both have hopes of attending college in the area, and I know that we are meant to be together. Matilda has confirmed this," he pauses momentarily.

Matilda has the ability to see souls, and souls that match to join into one. She was able to convince Sophia that Nate and she belong together. Sophia wanted to find someone to love, someone that her soul would match with for so long. When Nate came into her life she found that in a mortal.

Matt continues. "The past year has been full of secrets and difficult situations, but we have made it through each and every one of them. We'll make it through this as well. Ebony Triggs, I'm hoping that you will make me the happiest man alive. I love you with all my heart, as I will our baby. Will you marry me?" Matt slowly kneels before me and holds up a beautiful ring.

The tears flow down my face yet again–I am surprised there are any left. In shock I look around the room, gazing into each and every face. I see the joy in every set of eyes, as they all wait for me to answer.

"Of course I will Matt!" Still in shock, I pull him up and kiss him. "This ring is so beautiful." It is a single solitaire diamond held by a braided yellow gold band.

"Well, it was your mothers. Your Grams gave it to me a few months ago. She wanted me to have it for when we were ready. She knew we belonged together too."

The entire room erupts with cheers; Elijah pours champagne for everyone, and sparkling cider for me that Florence brings in from the kitchen. We begin to celebrate and I feel total peace with our situation. I know it will be hard, but what else is there to do? I can't believe the emotional roller coaster that I have been on the last month. Next month I turn seventeen, start senior year, and prepare to be a mother and a wife. This doesn't even include college applications and fighting *demons*. At least I have Matt and the Pierce family to support me. It is also time for me to realize that things are different when the supernatural is involved.

Constance smiles, "I'm so happy for you two; you are both handling this very well and with maturity. Teenage pregnancy is not something I think many could handle, and normally I wouldn't agree with marriage at such a young age. I mean, things have really changed in the last century or so; things just don't happen like they used too. But Matilda's ability to see souls helps us in knowing that the two of you do belong together."

"Thank you Constance. Normally I wouldn't pick teenage marriage and pregnancy as a great life choice either, but most teens are not *witches* or training to be a *guardian*. Life is already different for us and always will be, so why not be happy and start our life and family together now?" I give Matt's hand a loving squeeze.

As we celebrate I can't help but wonder how we are going to tell Matt's parents and everyone at school. I have come to terms with being pregnant, but I'm still concerned about what others will think. People like Mel pick on me already for being a *witch,* and she doesn't even know the half of it. I mean rumors are one thing, but if they only knew. All I need is for them to have more ammunition against me. And what in the world am I going to tell Eliza? She's going to kick me to the moon and back. I hope that my powers are not affected by the pregnancy, so I at least stand a chance against her. I'm even more determined now to banish Naberius, and soon; I don't want my baby to be affected by such black power as his. Maybe it's time to go home and talk with Eliza. I need to get this over with so I can concentrate on training and this new life inside of me.

♦ ♦ ♦

Matt takes me back to the manor, where we can talk to Eliza together. My emotions are jumping back and forth and I don't know if I'm coming or going, I'm so nervous right now. Eliza is not only my sister, but she has been like a mother to me, and she will be so disappointed in me. I can't blame her either–I can't blame anyone except myself; both Matt and I know better. There's no reason for us to get caught up in the moment the way we did. The fact is we are taught from a very young age always to use protection. They teach it in school, we see it on TV all the time, we know how important it is. I know all about teen pregnancies and sexually transmitted diseases. I also know that just because it's your first time having sex, it does not mean these things can't happen to you. Matt and I have proved that it can happen your first time. The more I think about it I can't help but wonder, what the hell were we thinking? I can't help but beat myself up over this, even though I'm pretty happy; the timing is just bad. I wonder if the change in hormones is making a rollercoaster out of my emotions.

Walking in the house I call out, "Eliza, can I talk to you?"

"Yeah. I'll be right there," she hollers from upstairs.

Matt and I take a seat in the family room, waiting for her to come down, when we hear the footsteps racing down the stairs.

"Hey Matt, hey Ebony, how was your night?"

With a quick glance at Matt, "Actually not too good, I was really sick last night and even Sophia couldn't help me."

"Are you okay now? I hope it's nothing major," she says with slight concern.

"I'm all right now, but it's kind of major. Constance took me to the hospital today to run some tests. That's what I want to talk to you about." I take a deep breath, and decide that the spill and duck method has been working out well so far. "It turns out that I'm about a month pregnant."

"You're what? Are you freaking kidding me? How stupid can you two be? You're sixteen years old Ebony, and I thought you were smarter than that! When you told me about having sex with Matt I assumed the two of you were responsible enough to use protection. Matt, I expected more from you; have you never heard of using a condom? Luke and I were just down the hall and there were two doctors in the house; did it ever occur to you to ask someone if you needed a condom? Even better yet, if you were not prepared, maybe you should have abstained!" She is so mad; I can see her vibrating as she yells.

"Eliza, we are aware that we made mistakes, but there's nothing we can do to change the past now," I defend as the tears build in my eyes.

"So what do you plan on doing? You're starting senior year, and I will not let you give up your education. The baby will be due in spring, just before graduation and finals," she huffs.

"You don't think we're aware of all of this? Florence promised to help us out. I am sure she will be willing to watch the baby for us when we go to school."

"So that means you plan on keeping the baby?"

Matt looks at Eliza, and begins to explain, "We don't have a choice. You should know better than anyone what this baby will be capable of. No one else would be fit to raise a baby with magical powers on both sides of the family. With Ebony being a *witch*, and me being a *guardian*, this baby will have the potential to be even more powerful than the two of you."

She flops back on the chairs as the realization hits her. "I guess I never thought of it that way. So what's next? What do we do now?"

"Well, because of the supernatural aspects, Constance has agreed to do a home delivery of the baby," I inform.

"Okay that makes sense; but in the next little while, I would like to sit down with Constance and discuss the possible complications."

With a half smirk, I admit, "I have one more thing to tell you."

"Don't tell me you're going to have twins."

"For god's sake, are you freaking kidding me? I'm not even sure if I can handle one."

Sitting here playing with Mom's ring that Matt gave me, I know this is going to be another huge shock. I just hope that Eliza isn't upset that I got Mom's ring instead of her. Matt and I getting married is the right thing to do. We're just lucky that we actually love each other and want to be together.

"Well, Matt and I are getting married." I hold up my hand and show Eliza the ring.

She buries her face in her hands, "Have you guys thought about school? What about college next year? I understand that you two love each other and are trying to do the right thing, but rushing into things is not necessarily the right thing to do. You can have the baby and still have options."

"I understand that you're worried; we are too. Just understand that I know this is right. Earlier today, when Constance was doing the ultrasound, Mom, Dad and

Grams came to me. They have shown me support and I hope you will too. I know this is not the ideal situation, but this is the situation Matt and I are in."

"Okay, I'm sorry. You have to understand, I am the only one left to protect you, and I have already failed." Eliza starts to cry.

I get up and go sit by my big sister, "You did not fail Eliza. Matt and I did this all on our own. I hate to break it to you, but it really had nothing to do with you."

Eliza and I sit there in each other's arms, both with the freefall of tears, but knowing that this will be much easier than some other things we have had to face in our lives.

# CHAPTER THIRTEEN
## Troubles

So much has happened in the past couple of months. From Grams death, to my pregnancy and engagement; I still can't believe that Matt's parents are handling everything so well. Now that school is back in full swing and Halloween is almost here, we need to concentrate on Samhain. I remember Grams saying it is one of the most important of the Sabbat's to a *witch*. Our new year, a time when the veil is the thinnest and making contact with those who have passed on is easiest. It's also a great time for us to release all that has happened this past year and plan for a new one. I need this more than ever, and need to cleanse myself and prepare for what is to come. This year, Eliza and I will hold a ritual that will include Matt, Luke, Nathanial and of course the Pierce family. After Samhain it will be time to focus on destroying Naberius. We want to make sure that we face him, before I am too far into my pregnancy and therefore vulnerable.

Sitting in the courtyard at school is so peaceful; leaves on the trees are starting to turn the most beautiful rust color before they perish for the year. Flowers are still in bloom and the grass is a lush green. Sophia once told me this is the most beautiful time of year; it's starting to cool down, but nothing has died yet. I have to agree with her. I enjoy just sitting here watching everyone walk by and wondering what is going through their heads at this very moment. Then I see the most beautiful sight of all walking towards me, my fiancé Matt.

"Hey beautiful, what are you doing out here by yourself?" He wraps his arms around me.

"Just enjoying the scenery and thinking about Samhain. Although I would much rather enjoy the company of the best looking man on campus."

"Well, if you point him out to me I can go get him for you."

With a smack I say, "Ha ha you're so funny, like I haven't heard that one before. Will your parents be joining us for Samhain this year?"

"I don't think so. I believe they are meeting up with a few friends, but I know they are grateful for the invitation."

"It's okay. I'm sure we have much more time for special occasions together."

Before we know, it is time to return to class and the masses start to rush inside the school doors. I'm glad schools almost over for the day, because Eliza and I have a lot of work to do tonight. We've been tracking a *succubus*. The female demon of seduction has been targeting men in the area. Through divination, we were able to figure out what is causing so many men in Massachusetts to behave so poorly. Papers have been reporting stories of various men leaving their families and jobs, as well as draining their bank accounts, only to end up in the streets, destitute and suffering from memory loss.

While in English class, I go over my research on the *succubus*. I've learned that she can take any form to make herself desirable to her target. Not only will she take as much material possessions as she can, she can drain the soul out of her victim through intercourse. Feeding from the souls of unsuspecting men, she gains power. The purer the soul is, the more power she gains. Becoming involved with a *succubus* can cause deteriorating health, and sometimes even death. I believe that she is leaving these men alive in an attempt to trap Eliza, and me but we are prepared for her.

Quietly grabbing my cell phone and putting it on mute, I start to text Alexander. 'Are you sure you are prepared to throw yourself at the *succubus*? We're not even sure if she'll be able to tell that you're not a mortal and what effects she'll have on you.' *Vampires* still have heartbeats and breathe, albeit at a much slower rate than mortals. I have no clue if the *succubus* will sense this or not.

A few minutes later, I feel the cell phone vibrate in my hand. 'You don't need to worry about me. I have no soul or life force for her to feed off of, and from my understanding my day crystal prevents any other supernatural being from knowing about me. I promised to help you and Eliza, so I'll keep that promise.'

I still have a hard time believing my *vampire* friends don't have souls. I mean, Matilda can see their

103

souls, so they should know better. Maybe they are using the term souls metaphorically; maybe they mean a pure or heavenly soul. I don't know, it just bothers me I guess. They are some of the most caring beings I've ever met. Maybe they just like to play on the stereotype.

I still worry about how this *succubus* will affect Alexander. I have to be honest to myself and say that I'd rather have him help than Matt. Alexander and the rest of the Pierce family have proven to be such assets in our fight against evil. And knowing that Alexander can hold his own makes me feel more comfortable taking him on this mission. I also believe that his power of telepathy will assist in narrowing her down. The most difficult part will be knowing exactly who she is, and the fact that she can change her appearance at any time. As the clock slowly ticks by, I continue to take notes and doodle. I tend to get a little more distracted these days.

♦ ♦ ♦

Eliza is already at the manor waiting for us and preparing supplies for tonight.

"Hey Ebony, how was school today?" she asks as usual.

"Same as always Eliza; my mind has been elsewhere today," I reply with a hint of attitude.

"I'm sorry, I'm just trying to keep things as normal as possible. Oh, and Alex, thanks for coming to help."

"Anytime Eliza, you know that my family is always here to help you, as you have us."

I grab our backpacks and start packing the supplies Eliza has prepared. We go over the list of victims again just to see if we can find a pattern. From what we can figure most of the victims were last seen at a local pub, and usually alone. Eliza grabs her pendulum and the map of Boston so that we can scry for *succubus*. The last two victims were both in the Boston area; because it is such a large city we assume she's still there. The two of us sit at the table and concentrate all of our collective energy towards the pendulum concentrating on the *succubus*. The pendulum points us to a pub near Harvard, where Luke recently took a job. I can feel Eliza's energy drain as panic sets in for the man she loves. Pushing away from the table, she quickly runs to the phone.

I give Alexander a nod and he connects us telepathically to Eliza as she calls Luke.

As Luke answers the phone Eliza asks frantically 'Luke, do you work tonight?'

'Yeah, I have to be there in about two hours. Why, what's up? Is everything okay?' His concern is evident.

'Okay, we will be there before you start work. The *demon* that I told you about to watch out for...'

'Yeah, what about her?'

'We have tracked her close to the pub that you work at. We assume she'll come there since it would be prime pickings. Please promise me you will be careful. Are you wearing your basketball ring?'

'I always do, except when I'm playing. Do you think the protection spell that you put on it will hold up?' he asks.

After Eliza confessed everything about us to Luke, we placed a protection spell on his State Championship ring, just as we did on Matt and Nathanial's gifts at Christmas. So far the spell has proven to be very helpful.

With a big sigh of relief Eliza says, 'There is no reason that it shouldn't. But please keep an eye out for anything suspicious. We'll get there as soon as possible. I love you.'

'I love you too. Don't worry. I'll be careful.'

She comes back into the room and starts grabbing the bags.

Alexander puts his hand on her shoulder. "We'll take my car Eliza. It's faster than yours, and I'm a faster driver. Not to mention this has just upped the ante for you and I think you are too emotional to drive," he insists.

"Thank you Alex, now let's go. I want to make sure we're there before Luke."

We finish loading the car and hit the highway as fast as Alexander's car allows us to. At this rate, we should be there in fifteen minutes, which is barely a fraction of the normal time it would take.

# CHAPTER FOURTEEN
## Succubus

"Why don't we take the booth in the corner? It gives us a full view of the pub," Alexander suggests.

"That's a great choice. It's also a little darker so we can use the crystal that we charged to detect the *succubus*. If and when she enters, the crystal will set off a glow," I explain.

Eliza takes the tea light out of the candleholder on our table and places the crystal inside the holder. This way it will only appear to be the glow of a candle. We seat ourselves strategically, with Eliza and me next to each other. Alexander sits across from us to make it appear as though he just came over to chat with a couple of girls. Shortly after she comes in Alexander will leave the table to sit at the bar, making it appear like he's struck out.

Luke walks in, just before seven o'clock, for his shift. With a slight nod, we know that he's prepared. As we wait we try to set up a plan and all agree that the faster we can get her to attach to Alexander and get them both out of the pub, the better. We don't want any of the innocent people that are here to have a good time to get stuck in the middle of our fight.

Out of nowhere the most beautiful woman I've ever seen walks in. She's tall and fit, with long black hair and dark olive skin. She boasts so much confidence that everyone in the pub stops what they're doing and notices her.

"That's the one," Eliza smacks me and we both notice the crystal glowing.

Alexander looks to us and sees the crystal aglow, and with a wink he tells us he's ready. Once Alexander finishes his drink, he stands up to bring attention to himself and says, "Thank you ladies. It was a pleasure to meet you; I hope you enjoy the rest of your evening." He then turns around and heads towards the bar, perching himself on a stool away from other patrons.

With a few whispers and some annoying giggles, Eliza and I act like a couple of tipsy college girls. Alexander ensures that we are connected telepathically, as well as Luke, to ensure that we all know what is going on. While at the bar Alexander pretends to confide in Luke in hopes that the *succubus* will be listening as she tries to make her mark. Alexander is playing his role perfectly. Even though physically he's extremely handsome, he is playing the role of the lonely, insecure man, telling Luke how he's new to town and has no friends or family, and is hoping to meet someone who'd be willing to show him around. I can't help but think that he is working the perfect hook.

Eliza and I both keep an eye on the tall dark beauty; she looks around nonchalantly before making her way around the pub. Slowly she begins to move closer to the bar, and as she approaches Alexander she asks, "Is this seat taken?"

"I was saving it just for you. Hi, my name's Alexander." Like the gentleman he is, he stands up and pulls out the bar stool, and helps her on.

"Thank you, it's nice to meet you Alexander. My name is Kyra. Would you be so kind as to buy me drink?"

"The lady's wish is my command. Bartender, can you please bring a lady a drink?" He gives Luke a wink: a hint to Luke to add the weakening potion into her drink that he had slipped to him earlier.

It doesn't take long for Kyra to make her move and try to get Alexander out of the bar. "I've had a lovely evening with you Alexander, but I must say it's time for me to go. Would it be forward of me to ask if you will be a doll and escort me to my place? It is getting late and I must admit I'm slightly impaired, and don't feel safe walking the streets by myself."

"Why of course, what kind of gentleman would I be if I allowed a beautiful lady like you to walk home alone?" He leans over the bar and shakes Luke's hand, "It is nice to meet you, man. Maybe I'll see you again sometime soon."

Alexander helps Kyra with her coat and they leave the bar together. Walking up the street we stay a few steps behind them, giggling and pretending to be a little drunk. After a few blocks, when nothing seems to be happening, Alexander telepathically suggests that we hang back a bit. Almost instantly, she leads him down a back alley, pushes him up against the wall, and begins to kiss him. Alexander turns around and slams her against the wall, grabbing her by her throat. Eliza and I come running around the corner to assist.

The three of us watch as she takes a true *demon* form. Dozens of razor-sharp teeth protrude from her mouth, and her beautiful long hair disappears as her weathered and rough skin takes over. Large pointy ears protrude from her head and her big beautiful brown eyes become sunken in, black and beady; from a beautiful exotic woman no one could take their eyes off of, to a hideous beast with a high-pitched squeal. She pushes Alexander down. As fast as he was on his back, he jumps to his feet. As they partake in a physical battle, Eliza and I begin to chant.

By the power of the moon,
we remove you
from this time,
and we banish you
from this place.
With the power of the moon,
we send you back,
never to leave a trace,
so mote it be,
so mote it be,
so mote it be.

The three of us huddle together and cover our ears as her bloodcurdling squeal echoes through the night air.

110

She combusts and is gone, leaving only Alexander, Eliza and myself in the alley. I feel a sense of relief that no more men will suffer at the hand of this *succubus*. I notice a scorch mark lining the old brick and mortar wall. The blackened mark outlines where the *succubus* was standing, I can't help but smile at the thought of all the men we helped tonight. Past victims will at least regain their memories and mental states; unfortunately, any of their financials are gone for good.

We go back to the pub so that Luke knows everything is okay.

"I was starting to wonder what took you guys so long," Luke confesses.

"It's no big deal. It just took a little longer for her to take the bait, but it's all over now," Eliza confirms.

"Thanks for your help tonight Luke. I wish we could stay longer, but I'm exhausted. The baby is sucking all of my energy out of me. I think it's time for us to head back to Wenham," I admit.

Eliza leans over and asks, "Ebony, are you okay if I stay here with Luke tonight?"

"Of course, I'll be fine. Alex will get me home safely. See you tomorrow."

"See you guys; have a good night." Alex waves as we leave to go home.

The car ride back to Wenham is just as fast as the drive out. Getting back to the manor, I make myself a cup of tea, crawl in to bed and call Matt.

He answers on the first ring, "I'm glad you called. I've been worried about you all night."

"I'm sorry; I never mean to worry you. I'm exhausted, but had to let you know that I'm back and miss you."

"I miss you too. It won't be much longer until we're together all the time. Then you'll be sick of me," he jokes.

"I could never get sick of you, especially if you get up for the three in the morning feedings and diaper duty."

"You know I will. So I'm thinking we should talk about setting a wedding date and whether or not you would like to make things official before the baby arrives."

"We will; why don't we sit down this weekend, and figure things out?" I suggest.

"That sounds like a great plan to me. Now you need to get some sleep, take care of yourself and our baby. Is Alexander staying the night with you tonight? You know, I don't like you being alone."

I giggle, "Yeah, he is and Mati is already here with him. You have nothing to worry about; I'm in good hands here. Now, let's both get some sleep. We have school tomorrow. I'll meet you there okay?"

"Okay, sweet dreams," he says with such sincerity.

"I love you, Matt. Have a good night and make sure you dream of me."

"I always do; I love you too."

Picking up one of my Wiccan history books I decide to study a little more; we need to learn some more basic witchcraft. We have concentrated so much on learning spells and potions that I think we have just skipped over the simple things. I want to learn more about such things as gemstones and the use of nature and herbs for things other than potions and spells. Grams taught us about some of the tools that we can use such as wands and athames. She also taught us about the various deities. The *gods* and *goddesses* are such an important part of Wicca that I think it is time to include them in our lives a little bit more.

Matilda comes in to check on me, "Hey kid, how are you feeling?"

"Pretty good, I just thought it was time to maybe learn a little bit more about my heritage and what we believe."

"So what are you up to?" She sits down next to me.

"Did you know that every color has a meaning, and every day of the week has a color?"

"I knew there were always reasons why you used certain colors of candles during your spells and rituals," she admits.

"Have you ever noticed a colorful glow around a person when you looked at them?"

"Yeah, now that you mention it, I have. What is it? I just assumed it was my eyes playing tricks on me, or an extension of the souls; maybe something I haven't learned yet."

"Yeah, I thought it was just my eyes too, but I was just reading in here about auras."

"So what exactly is an aura?" Matilda inquires.

"It's actually really cool. An aura is a visual manifestation of power," I explain.

"So if we learn to read auras, we should be able to gauge how powerful others are," Matilda confirms.

"Yes exactly!"

I'm betting that with Matilda's gift to see souls, this could be easy and beneficial to her. Something maybe we should all learn more about.

# CHAPTER FIFTEEN
## Acceptance

The sun shines through my window, and I roll over to look at my clock. Feeling the warmth beaming onto me, I feel excited about today; nervous but excited. How could anything go wrong on a bright sunny day like this? Noticing the red digital numbers–but they don't register– I just lie there, and soak in the beautiful rays. Suddenly, it clicks; I'm late. I'm supposed to meet Matt and his parents in thirty minutes at the pancake house on the other side of town. I jump out of bed and run down the hall to Eliza; she promised to come with me and help plan the wedding. I just hope she got home after staying the night with Luke.

"Oh, thank god you're here; we gotta go meet Matt and his folks."

"Oh, sorry kiddo I just got in."

"Okay first, you ever call me kiddo again there will be hell to pay. Second we need to hurry, so just get ready."

She chuckles as we both race out of the room and make ourselves presentable, before running out the door. Luckily we pull up right after them; Matt comes and opens my car door for me and takes my hand as we walk. I know his parents understand, but I am still nervous. We should be planning graduation, not a wedding and a family.

"Hi girls, it is nice to see you. I hope you're hungry," Mrs. Barton greets us.

"Thank you for inviting us," I respond.

"I believe that we need to make the best out of this situation. Plus, you are making me a grandmother, so I am indebted to you." She smiles and gives me a hug. "I don't advertise it, but I too was a young mother. I was only eighteen when Matt was born; Shawn and I married one month before his birth."

"I guess that explains why you understand our situation. Why didn't you tell me, Matt?"

"Mom only told me this morning. My parents wedding pictures only show them from the chest up; they worked very hard to hide things. Turns out she's two years younger than I thought. She told me she was twenty when she had me." He winks at his mom. "Every woman's dream, to turn back the birthday clock."

"Well, why don't we take this inside?" Mr. Barton suggests.

Thanks to the reservations Mrs. Barton made, we are seated immediately. As we are settling in the hostess takes our drink orders to pass on to our server. After a few moments of looking over the menu, we all agree on the brunch buffet. I have come to the conclusion that buffets should be served for every meal to every pregnant woman. Being pregnant, my appetite has increased tenfold, and it doesn't help that I'm completely indecisive about what I want to eat. It's nice now that the nausea has subsided, and I can actually keep something down. I do have to admit that from the books I've been reading, everything seems to be happening much faster with me than most women.

"So Ebony, do you have any ideas of what you'd like for your wedding?" Mrs. Barton pulls out a planner from her bag.

"There has been so much going on. I really haven't thought about it too much."

"Do you mind if I make some suggestions?" She asks.

"Not at all, I really have no clue what to do. From my family skills class the only thing I know is we need a marriage license. But other than that I don't know what else needs to be done," I admit.

"Ebony, I see Mrs. Barton has brought along a wedding planner; why don't we start there?" Eliza suggests.

"Yes, I brought this along because it has information about anything and everything you could possibly want or need for a wedding. There are multiple checklists that will help with keeping us organized."

"Thank you for helping us, Mom," Matt adds.

Throughout breakfast, we go over the various options for our wedding and try to narrow down a date. We decide without a doubt we want to be married before the baby arrives, and I would like it before I gain too much weight and the pregnancy is fully noticeable. Being that it's almost the end of October, and we do need a little bit of time to plan, we finally decide on December first for our wedding. We are going to have to work fast, since it's only four weeks away, but I know that we can pull it off with our family's help.

"Now that the date has been decided, I would like to suggest a handfasting ritual, since both of our families carry pagan beliefs," Eliza offers.

Matt's parents both smile in agreement, and his father adds, "We completely agree. Both of our families have strong beliefs, and we believe it is important to incorporate these beliefs."

Matt begins to share, "Alexander and I were talking about the wedding. The Pierce family has offered us the use of their home and beautiful garden for the wedding. I thought it might be nice to have the ceremony in their garden. Possibly in the gazebo, because I know how much Ebony enjoys nature and the outdoors."

"Matt, I must say your father and I have such pride that we have raised you to be such a gentleman. The fact that you want to be involved with planning this wedding, and that you have gone to the extent of coming up with options that would make a suitable choice pleases us both."Mrs. Barton glows with pride.

I start to feel emotional and sappy inside. I'm the luckiest pregnant teenager in the world; that is probably one of the funniest things I've ever thought of. Seriously, a lucky pregnant teenager, things can't possibly work out like this for most people in my situation. Yet my boyfriend didn't leave me, his parents haven't labeled me a Jezebel, and my family has not disowned me. In fact, it's the complete opposite, but that doesn't mean that I'm not scared, because I'm terrified. I still can't help but wonder how everyone at school is going to react, when they find out that I'm pregnant and Matt and I are getting married. I know the rumors will begin. I know that Mel will be the first one to start them. Mel is the head cheerleader and has been a thorn in my side for so long now, although since our altercation last year, she has been a little more discreet. I'm guessing that she is scared I will use my Jedi mind tricks on her again. I had to laugh when I heard her compare my powers to Star Wars, but whatever. Matt starts to rub my back gently. I know he can sense the tension and just the slightest touch from him helps to calm me. Maybe I should just come out of the broom closet, so to speak.

"Well, since there is not much time to plan for the wedding, I think we should contact the Pierce family about getting together and making arrangements. They have been so good to you kids. It is still hard for me to believe that they are so accepting of your supernatural abilities," Mrs. Barton says, not knowing about the Pierce family secret. This is even the first time she mentioned anything about me being a *witch*. I know Matt is close to his family and he told me that he explained about my family to them recently. Since Matt is a *guardian* in training, they are very aware of the supernatural, in particular *witches*.

"Yes we are lucky to have them. Many of the town's people have suspected that our family are *witches*, and base their opinions strictly off their suspicions, making them extremely judgmental of us; whereas the Pierce family is aware and knows about our history, yet they do not judge us," Eliza adds, knowing that the Barton's are unaware that our close friends are *vampires*.

"Matt," calls Mrs. Barton, trying to get her sons attention. "Maybe you should give them a call, and see if they are available today to meet with us and begin arrangements."

"I'm already texting Alex, Mom."

When we arrive at the Pierce house, Matilda already has the entire family room set up as if it was a wedding planner's office. I can't help but giggle; she is such a party planning freak, but she is great at it. The men all decide to go and hang out in the games room and leave us women to handle Matilda. Florence comes in with tea for all of us.

"Paige, Elijah and I would like to cover the costs associated with the wedding on behalf of Ms. Edwina. Being that it is usually the parents of the bride that covers expenses of a wedding and the fact that Ebony is like a daughter to us, we feel it is our responsibility and privilege to cover the wedding," Florence informs Matt's mother.

"Thank you Florence we appreciate the gesture, but it really isn't necessary. We don't mind."

"I know you don't, but this is something we would like to do for the kids."

"Well, I won't argue with you. Thank you again. Please let us know if there is anything that you would like us to help with."

"Thank you so much Florence, you and Elijah are too good to me and my sister." I jump up and give her a big hug.

We spend most of the day deciding on all the details for the wedding. Our invitations are a simple flat invite with a frosted transparent sheet on top. A light pink ribbon holds the two pieces together. Oh, and the flowers–I am so excited about the flowers! Five different shades of pink and various shade of white roses, calla lilies, Gerber daises and beautiful little white accent flowers will adorn the entire house. Intertwining flowers will cover the staircase railing and every door jam. There will be huge arrangements at the alter and around the large white tent outside. We also decide who will officiate for the service. Everyone agrees on a justice of the peace for the official ceremony, and Eliza will perform the hand fasting ritual. I think it will be perfect. We all agree to keep the wedding small. Matt's family, the Pierce's, Nathanial and Eliza, of course Matt and I as well. We will invite some friends from school, but will save the ritual for those who are close and important to us. I am hoping that Grams, Mom, and Dad will be able to make an appearance.

For my dress Constance has brought in a designer friend of hers from Boston. She has promised to make me the most amazing original dress for the big day. After about an hour of going through photos and talking, she says that she knows exactly what to do for me. I can't wait to see it; I'm really starting to get excited. I really want something youthful and timeless. I want to feel like a princess.

"I know I've said this a thousand times already, but thank you to all of you for your support. I believe that our wedding day will be a wonderful celebration of love. I know things have been rushed because of the baby, but I really do love Matt and I know he loves me." I let out a smile.

"We all know it too Ebony; this is meant to be. Although it may have happened a little sooner than expected, we know it's right," Mrs. Barton encourages.

# CHAPTER SIXTEEN
## Samhain

"So after the Halloween dance at school, we will meet out in the woods behind the Pierce house for Samhain, right?" Eliza confirms.

"Yeah, I'll be there about ten. Up at the meadow where we fought the Cerberus earlier this year; I know exactly where, so stop worrying," I insist.

She smirks, "I can't help it; you are still my baby sister and I want to make sure things are perfect. This is only our second Samhain ritual and being that the veil to other realms is so thin, I want to ensure everything is perfect. Make sure you are safe tonight, and please stay with someone at all times. I don't want any solo attacks tonight."

Samhain is the easiest time for *demons* to enter and attack. The veil between realms is the thinnest and the doorway opens.

"I know I'll be with Matt, Sophia and Nate all night. They'll be bringing me up to the meadow too. Who will you be with?"

"Constance and Isaac will both be helping me set up and cleanse the area."

"Luke isn't coming up tonight?"

"No, he has to work tonight."

With that Sophia shows up at the manor and we leave to get the boys for the dance that is being held in the school gymnasium. I think it will be fun. Danika joined the dance committee so we are very proud of her for getting out there and trying to stay in line. She has been working very hard to prove herself to the Pierce family. I can't imagine how difficult things have been for her; it has only been two years since her Embrace and not too long ago she was close to becoming a Cerberus. Now that she's aware of the dangers that lurk she is better prepared.

◆ ◆ ◆

"I sure hope that this dance goes a little better than the last one we all came to," Nathanial jokes.

Last year at the winter formal Nathanial was attacked by a rogue *vampire,* and would have died if Sophia hadn't healed him. He later remembered everything, forcing Sophia to divulge her immortal secret.

"Seriously, you're going to make jokes about being attacked by a *vampire*? If you're not careful, I'll be the next one to attack you." Sophia gives him a little nudge.

I can't help but giggle at their bickering; they're like an old married couple. "You know, I've always wondered something about the attack. Why did the *vampire* attacking the two of you use a knife?"

124

MYSTIC EMBRACE

"You know, that's actually a really good question. My guess would be, since he was such a new *vampire* he wasn't accustomed to his new abilities and still depended on his resources as a human. I got the feeling that he had mugged others before. He probably had the knife from his past life," Sophia explains.

Matt grabs both Sophia's hands and mine, leading us towards the dance floor. "Okay can we stop with all the bummer talk about attacks? I want us to try and have fun; this is my last school dance as a single man."

The dance goes by quickly and is a lot of fun. Danika and the rest of the committee has done a great job of planning. Who would've thought a bunch of high school students would go crazy over handfuls of candy being thrown into the crowd?

"Danika, would you like a ride home?"Sophia offers.

"Nah, I'm okay; some of us are going to stay behind and take down all the decorations. Just clean up a little bit, get things back to normal. I've already talked to Elijah, and he is going to pick me up when I text him. You guys go have fun with the ritual; I'll see you at home later tonight."

As we're walking back to the car I whisper to Sophia, "It's really nice to see you and Danika getting along a little better."

"Yeah, it makes the life at home a little easier," Sophia admits.

◆ ◆ ◆

Walking the path up to the meadow, I get a chill. It is almost as though something has passed straight through my soul. I've never had a sensation like this before; I turn to Alexander, wondering if he senses anything.

"Did you…" I begin to ask.

"No, I can't sense anything outside of our group and the animals in the area," he quickly answers.

"What's going on Ebony, are you okay?" Matt worries.

"Yeah, I think everything is okay. I just have this really strange feeling. It must have something to do with the baby; having something growing inside of you put's off some weird sensations."

It doesn't take as long to meet Eliza, Isaac and Constance in the meadow. They already have everything set up for the ritual. Now that we're all here, Eliza casts the circle and begins the ritual.

"Tonight we call upon the *spirits* of Wenham, Massachusetts in peace and in light. We invite them to walk among us. Tonight we call upon the *spirits* of the water, air, fire and earth. We ask thee to lift thy veil between realms and allow the gates between the worlds to be open wide. We come to celebrate the New Year and remember those who have gone before us. We call upon you to accept our offerings on this sacred night of the New Year. May you bless us in the year to come."

Eliza lifts up all of the sacred harvest fruits and vegetables in offering to the *gods* and *goddesses*.

"With the gates open, we call upon our ancestors, those known and unknown, to celebrate with us and guide us into the New Year."

She continues with the ritual and a small feast in honor of the celebration. Throughout the ritual, we see and feel various *spirits* around us; the feeling is absolutely unbelievable, to be surrounded by so many of our ancestors. We can learn so much from them. Once the ceremony is complete, Eliza closes the ritual.

"We thank you *spirits* for coming among us in peace and blessing our rite. Join us in peace, as we walk into the New Year. We thank our ancestors for coming among us, and remember you in love, for you will one day join us again, and we wait for your return. Blessed be."

"Blessed be," we all repeat

Eliza passes around paper and pens, "Now I invite you all to write down anything you would like to let go of from the past year. Once you're finished concentrate on it and throw it into the fire, watching it burn and the smoke rise, leaving us forever."

We each take a turn, happy to release some the negativity that has surrounded us for the past year, and start this New Year with peace.

As the ritual comes to a close Eliza reopens the circle. Everyone assists in cleaning up and restoring the area. I have to admit it's nice to have *vampire* friends. They are very quick and very strong, and help load the cars with all the supplies in no time. After one more sweep of the area, we start back down the path towards the cars.

All of a sudden I get the strange feeling again. It almost feels as though I'm floating, walking on air.

"Umm, Ebony," Matt tugs on my hand.

"Yeah, what's wrong?"

"I think he is concerned that you are about a foot off the ground," Eliza points out.

"What the hell are you...?" I bark back and look down, only to notice she is right. The entire group is staring at me.

"I guess this could explain the funny feeling I keep getting, but how is this possible? I'm telekinetic, I can't levitate."

"Well apparently you can now." Matt lets go of my hand and gives me a little push.

"Hey, what the heck are you doing? I am not a beach ball," I joke.

"Yet!" Sophia shouts as she runs up and gives me a little push.

They have their fun playing with me as I float slightly off the ground. It doesn't take much for me to concentrate and ground myself.

"Now you're all in for it." I start chasing after them.

It is not fair playing tag with *vampires*; they are just too fast and like to sneak up on me.

"This isn't fair!" I shout with a laugh.

"Aw muffin, too bad. This is how we *vampires* have fun, teasing our prey," Isaac jokes.

"Oh, so we're prey now, good to know. Maybe I should start carrying garlic," Matt shoots back, knowing that garlic doesn't actually ward off *vampires*, but he enjoys playing into the classic stereotype.

We goof around for a bit down the path before reaching the cars, but I think it may be time to get back to the manor and find out what is going on with me floating. Everyone decides to come over to our place; they want to know what's happening as well. Maybe I can even learn how to control it a little. I start to get excited over the possibility of a new power.

# CHAPTER SEVENTEEN
**Power Confusion**

Walking into the manor, Eliza quickly goes to the office for the *Book of Shadows*. Hoping that we can find some information about gaining new powers she flips through the pages. Constance goes to the kitchen and brews some tea, as Matt tries to help me understand my new power.

"Okay, so tell me exactly what you felt before we noticed you levitating." Matt takes the pen and paper Sophia grabbed for his notes. Matt takes note of everything, like the good little *guardian* student he is.

"Well it's kinda hard to explain. When we were first walking up to the meadow I had this feeling as if something was passing through me. It only lasted a moment."

He jots down some notes. "Now, what about when we were heading back to the car?"

"Well, it was the same feeling, and that is when you told me I was levitating."

"And how did you make it stop?" he asks.

"Not really sure. I just concentrated and focused my energy and willed myself to the ground," I admit.

"Have you ever had this feeling before?" Isaac asks.

"Nope, never, and the weird thing is that it happened at almost the exact same spot of the pathway both times."

Constance comes back in with the tea, "So, are you guys making any headway?"

"Not really, but it's kind of interesting," Sophia admits.

Eliza jumps up and slams the book on the table, pointing to a page. "Here we go, I think I got something," she says with excitement. "It says here that we can gain powers as we improve on our original ones. Also, sometimes during pregnancy a mother, *witch* or mortal, can absorb her baby's powers. So it appears that a mortal mother can give birth to a magickal being, just the opposite of our mortal father and a magickal mother."

"So we just have to find out if it is me or the baby."

"Well, there is another option too, and not as favorable."

With slight concern I ask, "What is not a good option?"

"Well, basically it says that if you enter an area occupied by a *spirit*, you can sometimes adapt to their powers."

"That doesn't sound too bad," I breathe a sigh of relief.

"That's not all; if the *spirit* finds you favorable, they can attach themselves to you and take over," Eliza explains.

"Okay, and which one of these options do you think happened to me?"

"I don't know for sure, but it sounds like the *spirit*. Because of the feeling you received of something passing through you, and the levitation occurring in the same spot, I can't help but think that it could be a *spirit* with tonight being Samhain and the veil being so thin. You have to admit, it makes sense." Eliza sits next to me.

I can't help but wonder if a *spirit* attaches itself to me, can it harm the baby? I don't know what to do. This baby has only been growing in me a few months and I love it so much already.

"Matt, there has to be some way we can figure this out. We have to protect our baby and I'm scared the *spirit* will harm it."

"Don't worry Ebony, we're going to protect our baby. *Spirits* can't harm you or the baby. If a *spirit* attached to you, it is only because it needs your help. Would you harm anyone you want help from? Plus we don't even know for sure that it is a *spirit*," Matt tries to calm me.

"Why would a *spirit* need my help?"

"Let's just try and find out if that's what it is before we figure out why it needs your help," Eliza suggests.

"How exactly do you suggest we find out if it is a *spirit* or not?" I ask.

"I think the easiest way is to use divination; we can use the Ouija board. This is a tried and tested way for us to speak with a spirit. Matt, would you mind getting it out of the office in the bottom drawer of the desk?" Eliza begins to clear the table.

"Is there anything that we can do?" Sophia offers.

"Just being here for support–you never know when we may need some muscle," I joke.

Matt comes back with the Ouija board and we try for almost an hour to contact the *spirit* attaching itself to me. Nothing happens, which proves that no *spirit* is attaching to me. This leaves my powers growing, or the baby is projecting its powers.

"Ebony we'll figure this out somehow. At least we know it is not a *spirit*, so this is good news," Eliza encourages.

Matt also tries to comfort me, "I know how hard this is for you Ebony, not knowing what is going on and having no one to talk to that has been through it. I wish there was something more I could do to help."

"It's okay Matt; I'm not the first teenage *witch* to go through pregnancy. I am just a little extra emotional these days."

"Just know that I am always here for you and my parents are too. Because of my family's history they are very understanding of anything supernatural."

"I know, and thank you."

The Pierce family decides to return home, and Matt calls his parents to explain what happened. They suggest that he stay the night, just to ensure I am alright. I feel so blessed to be gaining such a wonderful family.

Maybe tonight Matt can help Eliza and me with our lessons. Soon I will be in my second trimester of my pregnancy and it will be time to go after Naberius. It is time to increase training and begin preparations, assuming he continues sending his minions instead of coming after us himself.

"So where should we start?" I ask.

"I think we should work on strengthening your existing powers. Ebony, we'll work on increasing your telekinetic abilities, and Eliza we will work on strengthening your time control," Matt suggests.

Eliza's powers have progressed a lot faster than mine; I assume because she is a few years older than me. Her first power was time control and from there she has learned to astral project. I like this ability; she has used it to take me with her to alternate realms. It isn't really a new power just an extension of her time control.

Eliza sneaks behind Matt, poking at either side of his waist, "You're the boss, soon to be brother-in-law. Okay, so what activities do you want us to do?"

"Well for starters, instead of just freezing time, I want you to concentrate on strictly slowing it down. This is similar to what you do when you're astral projecting yourself. I want you to do the same thing, just stay here."

"Hey, what can I do? I don't really understand what I can work on. I move things, what else is there to do?"

"There's lots of things you can do Ebony. One thing I want you to try though; moving something and then changing directions. This will be handy when in a fight; you can even work on using multiple weapons at the same time."

We work on Matt's skills and exercises until the sun comes up. Matt's a really good teacher; everything that The Great Ones have taught him, he is using to help us. He's doing his job as a *guardian* even before his time. I don't want to think of the day that I lose him, but I know that he is going to be a great help to the lucky *witch* that has him for a *guardian*.

The thought brings me to ask. "I love having you help us, but I'm just wondering if we'll ever get our own *guardian*?"

"When you need your guardian the most, he or she will appear to you. I am guessing that since you had your Grams to guide you, the Great Ones must not have felt you needed one. Then right before she passed your parents came to you, and after her passing she came to you. Not to mention me; you two have more people to teach and guide you than anyone could hope for. You have no need for a *guardian* right now, which is not a bad thing," Matt explains.

"Okay Ebony. I think you need to get some sleep. We've been working all night, and you have a little one that you need to think of. My little niece or nephew needs to grow and their mommy needs to get some rest. Okay, so Matt, you should take my baby sister upstairs and get her tucked into bed. I'll bring up some warm milk for both of you," Eliza orders

"Who am I to argue with the big sister? You heard the lady, let's get you upstairs to bed." He scoops me up in his arms and carries me up the stairs.

136

"You know I can walk, right?"

"Yeah but who knows how much longer I will actually be able to do this." He smirks as I give him a little swat to the back of his head.

# CHARLOTTE BLACKWELL

# CHAPTER EIGHTEEN
## Final Preparations

I can't believe that tomorrow, I'm marrying Matt. The most amazing man in the world will be my husband in just over twenty-four hours. Realizing how much I actually have to do today, I jump out of bed and begin to get ready. Once I finish dressing, I fling open the curtains in my room. It is then that I see the ground is covered in snow; it is the most beautiful sight I've seen in a long time. Everything looks as though it is covered by crystals. The way that the bright golden sunrays touch each facet of every snowflake makes the sight breathtaking. I hope that it lasts until tomorrow. The frost on the trees and fence warm my heart, giving me the feeling of the perfect winter wonderland.

"Hey baby sis, you ready to go for your final dress fitting?" Eliza asks.

"You bet I am. Is Sophia here yet?"

"She just texted me; she'll be here any second."

Sophia pulls up just as we are walking out the door–her timing is impeccable. We jump in the car and are off to the seamstress. I'm so happy she was able to alter the dress Constance had made for me to fit my growing belly. I don't think I would have ever found anything quite so perfect.

Once we get the dress, Sophia pulls out the to-do list and begins to review everything we need to do. Florence is taking care of the flowers, cake and the catering. Sophia, Eliza and I are off to the day spa for mani/pedi's, facials and massages.

"Danika, Constance and Mati are meeting us at the spa. Are you ready for a day of pampering?" Sophia adds.

"You bet I am. What are the plans after that?"

"Our day is filled with relaxation. Tomorrow is a big day for our girl and we are here to ensure it is perfect," Sophia hints.

"But there is so much to do," I protest.

"And we have it all under control. The boy's are taking care of Matt and we even have a little surprise planned for the two of you later today." She winks at Eliza, and they both smile. I can't help but wonder what they are up too, but allow them this one without nagging.

The spa is beautiful, and the staff is so attentive. As we walk through the large glass French doors a young woman dressed in all white is there to greet us.

"Good morning ladies, welcome to Om spa. My name is Courtney. I will be your hostess today. So, who's the lucky girl?"

I slightly raise my hand as the others point to me.

"Well, let me start by showing you to your zen room. There are robes that await each of you. Once you've changed, I'll bring in some sparkling cider and fresh fruit with a chocolate fondue tray for your enjoyment. Later, after you've enjoyed a few treatments, I'll bring you lunch. You have a choice of fillet mignon or a beautiful stuffed chicken breast. I can also offer a vegetarian meal if any of you prefer."

She leads us to a beautiful room with white leather sofas and a spectacular waterfall wall. She lights dozens of candles around the room and lavender incense. There are six fluffy white terry cloth robes folded perfectly on a bench. Each robe has a sprig of lavender tucked under the belt. We each go into the changing rooms and change into our robes. Courtney already has the fondue tray and cider waiting on the table.

"Well ladies, I think it's best to get the worst over with first; this will allow you to enjoy the remainder of the day. Shall the bride to be go first?" Courtney offers.

"The worst?" I ask with concern.

She smiles, "Don't worry, it's not that bad. I'm just talking about the waxing. I think it is the least favorable of our treatments, although the lady we have is so good at what she does, it is almost like a mini massage rather than waxing. She is very gentle."

"Oh lucky me, I get to have another woman tear every extra hair out of my body. Sure, let's get it over with," I say with complete sarcasm., "The things we do for men."

Everyone including our hostess, laughs and nods at my comment. I follow her to a small room off to the side of the larger room we've been in. It's just as peaceful and tranquil as the first room. It doesn't take long for my waxing, and then the other girls go. Courtney shuffles us threw the various spa treatments. I can feel all five of us relaxing more after each treatment. I have to say my favorite so far is the Vichy shower, a light gentle massage with essential oils followed by a pressured shower that continues to massage every inch of my body as I relax on the table. This is wonderful; I have the best friends in the world.

"I just want to thank you for being such great friends to me. You support me through everything and are helping to make my wedding both special and memorable."

"Ebony, we all have had fun today," Matilda adds.

Constance smiles and grabs my hand, "Of course we support you and weddings are supposed to be special; just because you doing it a little sooner than we all would've expected doesn't mean that you don't deserve the best day possible."

"Well in that case we're off to a great start. So now that we're all pampered, where to next?" I try to pry.

The girls all giggle and just grab me by the hand to pull me off to the car.

◆ ◆ ◆

We pull up in front of the hospital, and I see Matt, Nathanial, Alexander, Isaac, and Luke all waiting outside.

"What are we doing here, is everything okay?" I begin to worry.

Constance smiles, "Everything is fine. Our next surprise has been difficult to keep from you. Today is your ultrasound. You get to see your baby, and the boys brought Matt here for it too."

"I don't think there's anything you guys can do to make this weekend any better. Now let's go see my baby!" I say with sheer excitement, as I jump out of the car and run into Matt's arms.

Our entire group enters the hospital and Constance leads us to the exam room, where the nurse already has everything set up. I change into a one of those blue, cotton hospital gowns and sit up on the examination table.

"Okay kiddo, lie back on the table and let's see what we can find." Constance covers me with a blanket and slightly lifts my gown. "This is going to be cold." She squeezes the gel onto my tummy and begins to move around the ultrasound probe.

Matt sits next to me and holds my hand, "I can't believe we're going to get to see our baby," he whispers.

As Constance moves the probe around, she stops and holds it in one spot. We hear a soft but extremely fast tapping noise. Constance smiles as she looks at us. "Can you guys hear that?"

"Yeah, but what is it?" I ask.

"That's your baby's heartbeat."

"Seriously? That's the baby's heart; it sounds like somebody tapping their fingers on the table," Matt says with excitement.

I can't stop smiling. This makes it even more real, and a few tears start to roll down my face.

"Ebony, are you okay, what's the matter?" Matt asks as he wipes the tears from my cheeks.

"I'm okay, this is just so amazing. These are happy tears."

"Would you guys like to see your baby now?" Constance asks.

Matt and I look at each other and then around the room at the loved ones around us, each one of them bouncing with excitement. With a smile we turn to Constance and nod. She turns the monitor towards Matt and me, and then flips the switch. The screen turns from a black-and-white picture to a type of sepia color.

"Okay, let's see this baby in 3-D." She smiles as she begins to probe some more, pointing out each part of the baby. It's amazing it really is 3-D. I can tell exactly what it is... the head, the fingers that he or she is sucking on. Every little detail is perfect. Seeing our baby for the first time is the most incredible experience I've ever had.

"Would you like to know if it's a boy or girl?"

"You can tell that?" I ask.

"Sure can, just have to move the probe a little bit lower."

As Constance begins to move the probe it suddenly floats out of her hand and is suspended in mid air. We all erupt with laughter.

Eliza walks towards me and puts her hand on my shoulder, "I guess we figured out what caused you to levitate. It seems as though your little one does not want you to know if it's a he or she."

"Great, a troublemaker already," Matt jokes. "Must be a boy. Like father like son."

Constance turns off the ultrasound machine and begins to wipe the gel from my stomach.

"Ebony, you can go get dressed. I am going to go and burn a DVD of today's ultrasound for you."

"That's so cool; Mom and Dad are going to be so excited to see this." Matt gives me a quick kiss on the cheek.

Constance comes back into the room with the DVD. I suggest that Matt take it home and show his parents and he happily agrees.

The boys leave to the Barton house, and we girls head to the Pierce house. I'm excited to get there, and see how all the decorating and arrangements are coming along. I know that Florence will have everything perfect; she is a stickler for details, and I know not one detail will be missed. Tomorrow is going to be a very busy day. I just hope I can get a good night's sleep tonight and that my family will show up for the wedding tomorrow. Eliza and I will have a quick bite to eat at the Pierce house and try and help with any last-minute details before we turn in for the night.

# CHAPTER NINETEEN
## Tradition

The music starts to play and Eliza takes my arm to guide me down the grand staircase. I thought I would be nervous, but I feel nothing but complete joy and peace. As Eliza and I make our way down the staircase, I see Dad waiting there with his hand held out. We make our way around the staircase, and I see Mom and Grams as well. Eliza passes me over to Dad, and she continues down the staircase ahead of us, just as a maid of honor should.

"Thank you for being here Dad, it means so much to me," I whisper.

"We would not miss it for the world. I am just glad I can walk my baby down the aisle," he says with a hug.

"How is it that you are here, and I can feel you this time?"

"Today is special; the Great Ones helped us. They can return us to human form when they feel it is important enough. I guess they feel the union of a future *guardian* and a Magnificent One is an important day." He smiles and kisses me as we continue down the aisle.

We hit the last step, and I look up and see Matt standing before us. He's so handsome. I see the tears well up in his eyes as he watches me move closer to him. Without a word his arm stretches out and he reaches for me. I look at Dad; he smiles and nods, and then places my hand in Matt's and kisses my cheek. We take a few more steps to reach the altar and the justice of the peace greets us.

Matt has never looked more handsome then he does tonight. Standing before me in a three piece black Armani tux and his hair slicked back, he has a certain glow to him. I feel so beautiful in my white baby doll gown adorned with crystals that sparkle so much they could pass for diamonds. The floor length gown is perfect, and even hides the small baby bump I'm beginning to show.

"Thank you all for joining us on this special day. Today Matt and Ebony exchange vows to become one. If anyone has a reason these two should not be wed, speak now or forever hold your peace." He pauses for a moment and then continues with the ceremony. "Ebony, would you like to share your vows with Matt."

"Matt, from the day you moved here, I knew there was something special about you. You stood by me even when I tried to push you away. You were there for me when things started to change, and you supported me when Grams passed. I know we are young, and I know we have more challenges ahead of us, but I also know with you by my side I can do anything. You are my rock, and have made me the happiest woman in the world. This is a year of great change for us soon our baby will join us, we will graduate high school, and hopefully go to college. I know that whatever happens, we will do it together. When we're hand in hand, nothing will be able to stop us. Today, you become my husband and I your wife, our lives will now join as one. Thank you for all the love, joy, and support you have given me. I was born to love you. I love you now and for always." I take a deep breath, surprised that I actually was able to finish.

The justice of the peace turns to Matt. "Now Matt if you will please share your vows with Ebony."

"From the moment I met you, I knew I had found the only love that I would ever know and need. From this day forward, we walk together. I'll use my heart to shield yours from pain, and I will use my love to warm our home. Your beauty and your heart inspire me to do great things; the first of those great things to love you and the next to love our baby. Together we move forward in this journey of life and love. I know that we are young and that we have so much ahead of us, but together I also know we can accomplish anything. You have taught me so much and I look forward to learning from you every day of my life. From today, into eternity, I give you my love and my life. Thank you for loving me, as much as I love you. " His eyes shine like the stars above when he looks at me, and I can feel his love with every inch of my being.

We exchange rings, and complete the ceremony with a kiss. Everyone cheers and claps; as we walk down the aisle they throw confetti. We wait for our friends and family to come and congratulate us. Later tonight when our friends from school leave, we'll complete the handfasting ritual. Nobody knew my parents, so no questions arise by their presence, although many people knew Grams, so I'm confused as to why nobody questions my dead grandmother being at our wedding. I wonder if she is only visible to the select few that she wishes to be seen by. I guess I will have to ask her. "Grams, why isn't anyone questioning your presence?" I whisper softly.

"Because to them, I do not look like your Grams. It is the magick of the Great Ones again. They would never risk exposing any of the supernatural secrets," she quietly explains while congratulating us.

Matt and I thank our guests for joining us as everyone shuffles through the receiving line towards the outdoor heated tents for the reception. As we are preparing to enter the tent the lights dim and the small lights above go on to look like little stars shining in the sky. A spotlight shines towards the entrance, and I can hear Alexander over the speaker.

"Please join me in welcoming the newly joined Mr. and Mrs. Matthew Barton." He raises his glass and everyone follows suit as we walk through the door.

Matt leads me to the center of the dance floor and the music starts to play as Matt and I share our first dance as husband and wife. This entire day is like a dream; everything's so perfect, the kind of wedding every little girl dreams of. We decided not to have a big dinner, but servers are moving around the area offering the guest various canapés and beverages. The mellow music plays as the few guests mingle and pictures are taken over the next few hours.

Matt stands up, "Ebony and I would like to thank all of you for partaking in this special day with us; it's been amazing."

Our guests begin to leave and thank us for sharing our day with them. Once they're all gone we begin to proceed with the handfasting ritual. As we prepare the area I notice Grams, Mom, and Dad deep in conversation; they look agitated.

"What's wrong? Do you have to return to…well wherever you came from? I understand, I'm just so glad you could be here with Matt and me tonight." I lean in to hug them.

"Kiddo, we are glad we are able to be here too; we are all truly blessed to share this day with you. It's not that we have to go—we sense something is coming. Something is coming now; we must prepare quickly," Mom explains.

"Something is coming here, now? But there's so many people here, people I love might get hurt." I begin to panic.

"That's why we have to move fast and get everyone to safety," Grams insists.

We need to ensure everyone's safety, but there is not enough time to get them out of here. Whatever is coming is coming to the Pierce house now.

"We need to get everyone into a safe place, cast a circle so that nothing can get to them and place a protection spell around them," Eliza orders.

"We have a hidden room that is steel plated. That should be the safest," Elijah suggests.

The Pierce family, along with Nathanial, Luke, Matt and my new mother and father in-law, all retreat to a hidden room behind the grand staircase. Dad's *spirit* joins them as he can help protect them, but since he's not magickal himself, he would be no help to us. I still wonder if he has some magick in him, being with Mom and The Great Ones, but maybe it's just because they are soul mates and they belong together. I shouldn't worry myself with that right now; we need to get our loved ones to safety. Of course only Grams can convince the Pierce's to stay with Matt and the rest of them. They want to help us, but with Mom and Grams here with Eliza and me, we can handle anything.

"Has all the staff left already?" I ask.

"Yes they left about thirty minutes after the guests, and the cleaning staff is not scheduled until morning," Florence assures.

"Okay everyone go in the room, and Matt you cast a circle asking the moon goddess Diana for protection; since tonight is a full moon she is the strongest. Once you are encased in the circle we'll close the door and place a protection spell," I explain frantically.

Sophia hugs me, "Are you sure you don't want our help?"

"Your powers will not help against the type of evil we fight. Grams and Mom will add to our power," I whisper.

"Why is Matt casting the circle?" Danika asks.

"If for some reason you need to get out, he will then be able to open the circle. He knows what he is doing," I say as I shut the door.

Eliza and I join hands with Mom and Grams. Eliza takes her free hand and places it on the trap door; I follow by doing the same. The four of us begin to visualize a large wall of fire surrounding the secret room and all those inside. We begin to chant,

"Craft the spell in the fire;
Craft it well and weave it higher.
Weave it now of shining flame;
None shall come to hurt or maim.
None shall pass this fiery wall;
None shall pass No, none at all.
So mote it be,
So mote it be,
So mote it be."

"Okay, do we know what it is that is coming?" Eliza asks.

"No we only sense it getting closer," Mom persists.

"Do you know how much time we have?" I question.

"Not exactly, but it will be soon."

I never noticed her leave, but Grams comes in with changes of clothes for both Eliza and me, allowing us to change out of our dresses and better prepare for a fight. After she changes, Eliza quickly runs to the kitchen. She returns with the potions that we have left here, in case something like this would ever happen. Panic fills me; how can this happen on mine and Matt's day?

Before I have a chance to drown in my own self-pity, or we have a chance to prepare, three pale creatures appear from a magickal realm opening in the floor. They resemble humans, but you can tell they have no soul; their eyes are yellow and you can almost see right through them. They begin circling us, as if stalking their prey; their long arms, are almost snakelike trying to slither around us. These are the creepiest things we've faced thus far.

"Grams, what are they?" I panic as their arms come closer.

"Those my dear are *soul suckers*. They search out the best souls and kindest people and take their souls. Their long arms wrap around you like a boa constrictor until they suck the very life force out of you."

We four Triggs women stand back to back with our hands clasped, when suddenly *soul suckers* lurch towards us. Before we know it all four of us are floating high above, nearing the roof of eighteen-foot ceilings. I guess my little one wanted to give us a few extra moments. I use my power to move the freezing potion, throwing it at the creatures.

"Now, that won't hold them long," Grams announces.

As we levitate above the *soul suckers,* Mom and Grams lead us in a banishing chant.

"The power of the air,
the power of the earth,

the power of the water,
the power of the fire,
join together, all four elements,
and banish this evil night dweller.
So mote it be,
So mote it be,
So mote it be."

With conviction, we repeat the chant once more, and watch the *soul suckers* implode beneath us. This is possibly the scariest yet easiest fight we've faced yet. I can only imagine what may have happened had we not risen from the ground out of their reach. Slowly we float back down to the surface, and now we can continue with the handfasting ceremony, once we've collected ourselves. Eliza releases the protection spell from the hidden room, and we quickly open the door, to assure ourselves that our loved ones are safe. When Matt realizes that the coast is clear he opens the circle again. They all rush out, hugging us with relief that we succeeded again.

"Okay, it has been quite the interesting night; why don't we continue with the ceremony? I will not let anything ruin your day," Florence suggests.

"I think that's a great idea. I'm sure that Mom, Dad and Grams will need to get back soon," I admit.

Grams stands before us as a high priestess. "Matt and Ebony please join hands." The ceremonial rope on the alter in front of Grams rises and folds overtop of our joined hands. "With this rope I bind you."

Matt and I say together, "My heart, my body, I am yours forever more."

"Now you may seal your handfasting with a kiss," Grams raises her arms to us.

As we complete the ceremony, and our loved ones leave, Matt and I thank his parents and the Pierce family for the most wonderful day we could have ever asked for. Of course, fighting evil entities adds to the excitement. Isaac pulls Matt off to the side for a moment. I can see him handing him the keys to his sports car. I look to Constance with a questioning look, and she just smiles as Matt and Isaac come back.

I can't help but ask, "What was that all about?"

"Isaac has given us his car for the evening, and our wonderful friends have prepared a room for us up at the mountain lodge. Let's go celebrate our wedding together," Matt winks.

As we drive out fireworks begin going off above of us. The bright colors lighting up the night sky lead us into our future. The night has been magnificent and I can't help but be grateful.

"Those *vampires* really do think of everything," I chuckle.

# CHAPTER TWENTY
## Time Flies

I can't believe spring is almost here; the past couple months have gone by so fast. The baby is due in about a month and then graduation shortly after. Matt and I have had so much happen this year that it's hard to believe we're still happy. Most teenagers–most people for that matter–would be at each other's throats dealing with marriage, a baby, SAT's, college applications, and graduation. It is more than most people could handle. Today the boys are going for their tux fittings for senior prom; we girls get to go shopping.

"I think we should go in to Boston–they'll have better selections. Since the baby is due so close to prom I think I need something like a baby doll dress. Only God knows when the baby will come into the world; it could be late and come like two days before prom, and who knows if I'll have time to lose the weight," I start complaining.

Sophia chuckles, "I think someone's getting a little moody."

"You would be moody too. I have a miniature *succubus* growing inside of me and causing me to abandon my entire wardrobe for parachutes. I mean think about it; Kyra the *succubus* sucked the life out of the men she attacked, and the baby is sucking the life out of me. I have no energy or control over my appetite, bladder or sleep. So there we have it–I have a little *succubus* growing inside me. "

Matilda puts her arm around me, "Well sweetie, it'll be over soon. But for today, you have my amazing fashion sense and talent for shopping to aid you in your prom dress search."

We all agree that Newberry Street is the best place for our search. Sophia finds a place to park, and we begin our trek up and down the street on foot. With all these designer shops the three of us should be able to find something perfect.

"Okay Ebony, I think your mood is affecting my shopping mojo. We have been in almost every shop and not one of us has found anything yet. You need to cheer up. We all need to," Matilda mopes into the next store.

"What is it anyways Ebony? I have never seen you this miserable before," Sophia adds.

"I'm sorry. I guess this is just a bad day for shopping. I'm really not feeling that good, I'm kind of nauseous today, and my back is absolutely killing me."

"Maybe all this walking isn't a good idea for you. It's only a month until the baby is due we can always have someone bring dresses to the house for showing," Matilda suggests.

"Yeah, let's get you home." Sophia takes my arm as we walk towards the car.

Making our way back to the car, I get an awful cramp and double over, letting out a painful cry.

"What's happening Ebony, what is it?" Sophia asks in a panic.

"I don't know, it hurts so bad! I need to get home and lay down," I insist.

Sophia and Matilda help me back up and lead me towards the car. All of a sudden there is a gush of warm fluid that pours down my legs. Completely embarrassed by the fact that I just pissed my pants, I take my jacket and wrap it around my waist.

"We have to hurry; I just had a little accident."

The girls both turn to see what is happening. They share a quick glance with each other and then look at me slightly panicked. Sophia quickly places her hand on my stomach, looks at Matilda and nods.

"Ebony, we need to get you back to Wenham and you need to go to the hospital and get things looked at. You're over a month away from your due date and we need to know what is happening."

"No, I just need to go lie down. My back is hurting from all the walking, my tummy is hurting because I'm hungry, and I just pissed myself because the baby is pushing on my bladder."

"No Ebony. That's not what happened. Your back and tummy are hurting, because you're having contractions, and you didn't pee yourself–your water just broke. You, my dear,, are in labor and the baby is coming," Sophia explains.

"No it's too early; the baby isn't due for another month," I argue.

"Okay, let's get you back to town, and we'll have Constance take a look," Matilda suggests.

"I'll get looked at when we get back, but please don't worry about me. Really it's nothing, let's just go home."

The girls get me back to town in record time, driving directly to the hospital, ignoring my protests. Matilda calls Constance to tell her what's happening. She agrees to meet us there to do an exam. I hope these cramps will go away once I get something to eat; I don't know how much longer I can handle this stabbing pain. It doesn't take long for the hospital to get me into a room. Constance is already there and has a gown waiting for me.

"Ebony I want you to get changed into this, and I will be back in a minute to examine you. Do you need any help getting changed?"

"No, I think I'll be okay. This really isn't necessary Constance."

"Let me be the judge that."

A few moments later, she returns with nurse Kathi, "We are going to perform what is called a non-stress test. All it consists of is attaching these two little sensors on your tummy. One will monitor the baby's heart rate through a connection to this monitor, the other will monitor to see if you are having any contractions. I also want you to push this button every time you feel the baby move. This will take about twenty minutes to complete. I also want an internal exam to check if you are dilating and if it was your water that broke."

"How can you tell if it's my water that broke?" I question.

"I'm going to use this special cotton swab, if it turns blue that will indicate the presence of amniotic fluid."

Constance informs me that it is in fact, amniotic fluid. Because I'm still four weeks until my due date she wants to give me antibiotics to reduce the risk of infection, as well a steroids to help mature the baby's lungs. Once all is said and done, she informs me the non-stress test also proves that my pains are in fact contractions. She orders the proper medications and nurse Kathi leaves the room to retrieve them.

I begin to cry, scared for my baby, "Can somebody please call Matt?"

"Sophia's already calling him. Ebony I don't want you worry, everything is going to be fine."

"But the baby isn't due yet. It's too early, it is only April fifth."

"Actually it is almost the sixth, look at the clock. Time flies when you're having fun."

"It's not that early, we actually considered babies full term at thirty-seven weeks and you are almost thirty-six." Nurse Kathi explains as she puts in an IV with ampicillin. "Try to get a little rest, we are going to get everything organized, and I'll be back to check on you shortly."

Nurse Kathi along with Sophia, Matilda, and Danika all leave the room so I can try to get some rest.

As I try to calm myself. I begin to feel extremely warm; the air seems to thicken as it becomes harder to breathe. My palms begin to itch, followed by the soles of my feet giving me the feeling as if I was playing in poison ivy all day. I want to tear my skin off. As I move my feet around on the bed try to relieve the itching. I notice a slowing of beeping sounds and look at the monitor, and the baby's heart rate dropped from 160 beats per minute to 52 beats. Realizing that something is going wrong, I look for the buzzer to call the nurse, but I can't find it anywhere. My heart starts pounding through my chest as I reach for the phone, which also isn't there. I jump to my feet in an attempt to run and get help but the IV is attached to the bed, and I can't move more than two feet.

"HELP! Somebody please help me. Something's wrong," I try to scream as my voice cracks from fear.

Constance and Kathi both run back into the room, and frantically check the monitor as I explain what I'm feeling. Sophia and her sisters are right behind them. Constance pulls out this long wire and begins another internal exam.

"Ebony, I am attaching this wire to the baby's head. This will tell me with certainty if the baby's heart rate is dropping."

"What's happening? Is my baby going to be okay?" I begin to panic and cry even harder.

"I'm going to do everything in my power to make sure your baby is okay. I think you are reacting to the medication we gave you," Constance explains as Kathi quickly takes down the medication bag and flushes the line with saline solution.

"Okay Ebony, the baby is in distress, and we need to deliver you now. We need to do an emergency cesarean section, and get the baby out as fast as possible," Constance explains.

"But Matt isn't here yet."

"I know sweetie, but we need to do this now. I am going to take care of you and your baby." Constance kisses my forehead. "Sophia and Mati will tell him what's happening when he arrives. They can show him where we are, so he can wait outside the O.R.

Sophia nods in agreement.

Constance and Kathi push the bed down the hall, almost running, "Move, Move!" they scream.

All I notice is other pregnant women jumping back through their bedroom doors to get out of the way.

"Okay Ebony, I need you to move over to the operating table. I'm going to prepare for the surgery and the nurses here are going to prep you and help clean you up for the operation. We don't have much time, so we need to get you to sleep," Constance explains me.

The nurses begin to spray this rust color solution all over my stomach. As the doctor behind me injects a different medication into my IV line, which Kathi had capped and left in place.

He then says, "Ebony I am going to place this mask over your mouth and nose. I want you to breathe deeply and count backwards from ten. This is a combination of inhaled anesthetic and oxygen. The medication that I placed in your IV is also an anesthetic. You'll be asleep and won't feel anything during your surgery; you'll wake up shortly after it's complete."

I'm so scared; Matt isn't here. I didn't see Sophia outside and I'm scared something might happen to my baby. I notice Constance walk in with her hands up in the air and surgical gloves on. She smiles at me and nods. I don't think I've ever breathed so deeply in my life. I want to fall asleep as fast as possible so Constance can save my baby.

I begin to count, "ten, nine, eigh…."

# CHAPTER TWENTY-ONE
## Embracing

I hear Matt's voice, "Ebony, wake up honey. I have someone here who would like to meet you."

I slowly start to open my eyes; my throat hurts and my abdomen is burning, but I see Matt and smile.

"Hey beautiful, I'm glad you are awake now. You had us all worried."

"The baby, is the baby okay?" I ask anxiously.

"She is right here, and she is perfect." He brings the most beautiful baby I've ever seen up to my side; my heart melts.

"We have a girl, we have a daughter?" Tears begin to sting my eyes

"Yes, and she's just beautiful as her mother. Would you like to hold her?"

I lie in my bed holding the tiniest little girl, checking to make sure she's okay, counting ten fingers and ten toes. She has the creamiest brown skin and head full of dark brown hair, already showing off her curls. We sit and admire the beauty that Matt and I created; I hear the tiniest little squeak come out of her little mouth. I lean down and kiss her pink, full, perfect little mouth. "I love you baby girl." I feel a tear stream down my face.

Constance comes back into the room, "Ebony, we need to take the baby to the nursery for a checkup and the nurses will give her a bath. This will also give me a chance to examine you."

"Okay, can Matt stay with her though?"

"He sure can."

The nurse puts the baby in the little bassinet and begins to wheel her out of the room.

Matt turns to me, "Are you sure you'll be okay?"

I nod, and he follows the nurse and the baby.

"Okay I just have to press on your stomach. I need to check the uterus and make sure it is tightening. This might hurt a little because of the incisions." Constance explains.

As she firmly presses on my stomach pain shoots through every inch of me, and I let out a cry. I pull back on my emotions and try to meditate through the pain. I know Constance isn't trying to hurt me, and this needs to be done. She moves and palpates another spot; the pain is excruciating. I take a deep breath, as tears roll down my face. Then I get the sensation that I have wet myself again–it feels funny. I feel funny. Something isn't right. I look at Constance's face to try to gage her reaction, "Constance, what's happening? I don't feel very good."

She leans over to put another medication to my IV, "Sweetie, you are hemorrhaging. Your uterus is not retracting the way it should and you are having some bleeding. I know it's painful, but what I'm trying to do is massage your uterus in order to get it to contract. If I can't get the bleeding to stop in the next few minutes, I am going to have to take you back into surgery." She leans over me and pushes the call button asking for a nurse to come in to assist her. "I need you to stay calm, Ebony. I know that you are scared. I'm here, and I'm not going to leave your side."

A few minutes pass of Constance massaging my stomach. The pain is excruciating but I'm so terrified that I barely notice it. Constance and nurse Kathi are talking quietly in the corner when Matt comes running back in.

"What is going on? I was told you needed me back here immediately," he asks with sheer panic.

"Ebony hasn't stopped bleeding, and I need to take her back into surgery to control the bleeding. I don't want to scare you two but this is dangerous and I may need to remove the uterus, which would mean no more kids. Do you both understand?" Constance asks.

"Yes, just help her please!" Matt cries.

Kathi leaves the room and Constance whispers, "Do you want me to do EVERYTHING I can?"

"Of course," Matt and I agree.

"Do you think I may die? Matt I'm scared." My heart sinks deep into my stomach.

"I will not lose you."

With her hand on my shoulder, Constance swears. "I will make sure you wake up, no matter what. Now we must go."

Nurse Kathi comes back in the room; the two of them begin to wheel me back to the operating room.

Once in the operating room, the same procedure as the previous surgery happens and then I am out.

♦ ♦ ♦

When I wake up Florence and Elijah are at my side, along with Constance, Isaac, Sophia and Matt.

"Why is everyone here?" I ask.

"Honey, we had some complications during surgery," Constance begins.

"Oh my god, am I dead?" They all just stand there looking at me. "Oh I am! I guess this is just me saying goodbye before I move on," I say, not thinking any of them can hear me.

"It isn't that simple." Matt sits next to me.

"Why not? I don't feel pain anymore, I feel different." A sense of relief takes over; if Matt can hear me at least I'm still alive.

Constance brushes the hair from my face, "Well you are different; for one you are a mother. Although there is something else different too; you lost too much blood during surgery and we tried to transfuse you."

"So this blood you had to give me is what's making me feel different?"

"Not that blood. See, I did everything I could and we were about to lose you. I promised you I would do everything in my power and I did. I used my speed and gave you a small bite to allow the venom into your blood stream. I then gave you a few drops of my blood. I did all this without everyone noticing. Your heart was still pumping enough to allow my blood and venom to move through your system, thus allowing your vitals to stabilize and appear to the other members of the surgical team that you were improving. You are going through the Embrace and soon will be a vampire like us," Constance explains.

Sophia once explained that to turn a mortal into a *vampire*, they must still be alive and need a combination of venom from a *vampire* bite and then drink the blood of a *vampire*. This is called the Embrace, when a mortal life embraces the life of a *vampire*.

"What? So I'm dead, or at least will fully be soon. How is this going to work, what about Matt and the baby?" I begin to freak out. I know that *vampires* aren't actually dead, just immortal. They still breathe and have a heartbeat; just everything slows to a point where a mortal wouldn't survive. These natural actions are nearly undetectable to a mortal.

Matt takes me in his arms, "Ebony, it's okay. We'll make this work. I am just glad to still have you here with me. I need you, your sister needs you and our daughter needs you."

As Elijah sits down and goes over what I will be experiencing I just kinda shut down. So now not only am I a *witch*, but I am a *vampire-witch*. Or am I even still a *witch*? I'm so confused. My focus then turns to my little girl who I only saw for a moment; at least I will be here for her.

"I'm in complete shock right now; maybe we can talk about me later. I'd really love to see my little girl," I request.

Matt walks just outside the room for a moment and comes back in and sits next to me again. "Mommy, I would like to introduce you to our baby girl. Since we didn't have a name picked out, I've been calling her Peanut. She weighs only four pounds thirteen ounces, but she is very healthy and strong like her mama. You want to know something cool? She was born right at the stroke of midnight on the sixth. She stays in line to gain the magnificent power."

I reach out my arm to hold peanut for only the second time in her new life. I'm mesmerized by her beauty, and just can't believe she's here. So much has changed since Grams died. "Well I think we should name her. Can you imagine how bad she would get teased at school with a name like Peanut?"

"Do you have anything in mind?" Matt asks.

"I have no clue, to be honest," I admit. "Does anyone else have any ideas?"

Sophia smiles, "I do. I always figured if you had a little girl you would need a name that starts with an E— you know to stick with tradition."

"Okay, give it to us."

"Well I have two actually—Emalia or Elyn."

Matt and I look at each other and look at Peanut and both say, "Elyn."

"I love it Sophia, thanks. Hi, little Elyn, it is very nice to finally meet you. Welcome to the world." I give her a little kiss. "Constance, I feel funny, I'm hungry but the thought of food is making me sick."

Florence takes my hand, "That is your bloodlust setting in. I have something prepared for you, and you can take small sips of it. This will lessen the feeling you are experiencing."

"Ebony, just make sure you only take small sips at a time. You are still transitioning and if you drink to fast you will get ill," Elijah adds.

"Does Eliza know what's going on?"

Sophia receives a text message and after reading it, she says, "Alex and Mati have gone to talk to her now. They should all be back here soon."

"I didn't even notice them leave. I hope she's going to handle everything okay. We only have each other, and now—well, look at me."

CHARLOTTE BLACKWELL

# CHAPTER TWENTY-TWO
## New Home

Florence and Elijah have set up an entire wing of the house for me, Matt, and Elyn. They need to keep me close to ensure I handle my Embrace. I spoke with them the other day about what is to come and it appears that I still maintain all my *witch* powers. They may even become stronger now. Eliza's staying here too; we don't want her to be alone. It's great having so many people around to help with Elyn, but it is hard transitioning. I crave blood; I crave Matt's, and Eliza's, and even Elyn's blood. I want to drink my own family's blood. I am just thankful that Alexander is keeping such a close eye on me. He keeps telepathic lines open at all times to ensure everyone's safety.

I hear Eliza come up to the door. "Eliza I know it's you. I can tell by your footsteps," I chuckle.

"I just wanna come see that beautiful little niece of mine," she says as she enters my room.

"Of course, she loves her auntie."

"To be honest, I thought that I could watch Elyn for you. Elijah wants to do some training with you."

"That would be great, thanks." I smile.

"Anytime sis. So how are you handling your new life?" she asks.

"I think I'm doing okay; it is hard at times though. I'm so lucky to have so many people here to help me," I admit. "The best part is healing so fast; most women would still be in pain from surgery. I feel great physically, and look–I don't even have a scar."

"I'll always be here for you, no matter what."

"I miss the manor though. I'd like to go back there and pick up a few things. Since I was Embraced I haven't been allowed to go anywhere," I complain.

"I know it must be hard, but I'm glad you have been keeping up on your school work while you're here."

"There isn't much else I can do–I can hardly sleep."

"I think every new mother wishes she were like you and didn't need sleep to function. Elyn waking for feedings doesn't affect you the way it does others," she jokes.

Since *vampires* don't require much sleep, just a few hours rejuvenates me. Although most *vampires* tend to sleep during the day, to avoid being burned by the sun, the Pierce's and I still sleep at night, trying to keep up the mortal image. Of course, they also have their magickal day crystals.

"Yeah, yeah, but I think we are going to need to look through the *Book of Shadows* and find some spells that will prevent me from harming or feeding on innocent people. I'm scared all the time of hurting you, Matt or Elyn, and prom is in two weeks and I can't miss it. Soon we will have final exams and graduation. This is my high school graduation and it is important."

"I think that is why Elijah wants to work with you, to get you prepared for prom. He doesn't have the time frame to work with you that he had with the others."

"Well I better go, but will you look through the book and see what you can find?"

"Of course I will; maybe we should contact Grams too. I think it may be time to let them in on everything. Of course, assuming they don't know yet," Eliza suggests.

"Good idea. I better go, take care of my little Peanut," I say as I run down the stairs.

🔻 🔻 🔻

I get down to the family room and the entire Pierce family is there waiting for me. I remember what their fight training is like from when we took on the Cerberus, but also know this is different. I need to learn how to handle my newly increased senses, my thirst, and just normal daily living.

Elijah turns to me, "Hey kiddo, are you ready? Today we are going to work with your control. You never know when a mortal will get injured and bleed around you, so we will work around open human blood bags today. I want you to learn to control your response long enough to be removed from the situation." A *vampires* reaction to blood is also called bloodlust, but I've only heard the Pierce's refer to it that way once before. They try very hard to be civilized in every way.

"This takes a long time to learn. I still struggle with it, as you know from when Nathanial got injured and when his mom cut herself. You'll not perfect it like Isaac or Constance, but you will learn to get out of there; and fast, instead of feeding." Sophia reassures.

Last year Nathanial's mom cut herself and Sophia had to excuse herself from the situation. She blamed being sensitive around blood on the memories of Nathanial's attack. Later that night she confessed everything to Nathanial.

"Okay I'm ready."

"I have already talked to Eliza and Matt about this. Matt is at work and won't come home until he calls and hears that it's safe. Eliza has placed a spell so none of us can get into the room her and Elyn are in," Elijah adds.

"That makes me feel a little better. In case something goes wrong, I can't get to them."

"Exactly."

They begin by putting a blind fold on me. Various items are brought out for me to smell. The goal is not only to control my reaction to blood but also to food. Eliza and I already made me a day crystal, with the veneficus lamia sol solis partonus stone. This is the same black diamond Grams and her mother used to make day crystals for the Pierce family. When they returned to Wenham with Danika and needed one for her, Eliza and I helped Grams bless one. Now I have one of my own; who would have ever suspected we would need to make one for one of us? Alexander has a talent for making jewelry, and encrusted the stones in to a band that I wear as my wedding ring. Since Matt proposed with my mother's ring and we did not feel the need to spend extra money on a band, this works out perfectly. The two rings fit together like a perfect set.

"So how exactly does my day crystal work?" I ask as they wave the unappealing food in front of me and I pull away from the god-awful stench that makes me gag.

I hear Florence crack a smile, telling by the sound of her lips moving against her teeth and the saliva from her mouth. I have learned specific sounds everyone makes; the increase in my hearing has been the most difficult to deal with. I am glad that was the first thing we worked on.

"Well my dear, your day crystal helps with many things. The first and most important is you are able to go in the sunlight. It also helps with controlling your cravings to a point. Another important fact is you can eat regular food; this helps decrease suspicion among the mortals. Normally human food causes *vampires* immense distress, severe stomach pain, and it is not pleasant," Florence explains.

"Okay, now back to work. I want you to tell me what you smell, and try to keep a straight face," Elijah instructs.

"Okay, well this one is bacon, that's easy–and it smells revolting. It is so strong." I wince and turn my head.

"Yes, bacon is one of the stronger scents. Now don't turn away, just try to get used to it," Elijah encourages.

I sit as Danika waves the plate of bacon in my face. I get a sick feeling, almost as though I'm going to throw up. I can tell it is Danika by the tapping of her foot.

"You can do it Eb. The next one isn't as bad," Sophia encourages.

I try to fight through the smell, and it doesn't take long before I'm used to it. Just to be a smart ass I reach out and grab a piece, throwing it in my mouth and eating.

"Very good Ebony, I still can't eat bacon," Danika confesses.

They continue on with a few different scents, including flowers, perfume, food, and cleaning products. Then they bring out the blood; first animal then donated bags of human blood.

Isaac walks behind me and unties the blindfold. "Let's remove the blindfold. Now that you know how to fight through it when you can't see what you smell, you need to learn how to fight through it when you see what you smell too. This will be even more difficult with the sight of blood."

I can feel the burning in my eyes and throat. My chest feels as though someone poured acid on it. The human blood is so much harder to control myself around. I feel the ripping in my mouth as my fangs descend.

"It's okay, Ebony; when you feel this happening try your meditation techniques. Try to think of Elyn, anything to take your mind away from the blood and your thirst," Constance encourages.

Almost as soon as she says Elyn, I feel everything retract. I just think of my beautiful little girl, and of how I never want her to see me as a monster.

"I think I've found my calming tool," I say with excitement.

"That you have," Sophia agrees. "I still have nothing that works that good. You have only been a *vampire* for a few weeks, and I have been one for over a hundred years. You amaze me Ebony Triggs...ah excuse me, Ebony Barton."

"Well I kinda thought it would be Triggs-Barton-Pierce now," I joke.

"You have always been and will always be a member of this family, whether you have our last name or not," Florence says as she hands me a drink.

"Maybe we should take it a step further," Elijah suggests.

"What do you mean?" I ask.

"Matt called a few moments ago–I told him it was safe to come home. We can try to have the open blood with a mortal in the room."

"But...but...what if...?"

"We are all here to make sure he doesn't get hurt. You have a mortal husband and daughter; I think it is important. Little kids get cuts and scratches–you need to be prepared. For the safety of those you love," Elijah insists.

"I understand, but I'm scared." I look up just as Matt walks through the door.

I watch as my husband, the father of my child, enters the room and I try to remain calm. The temptation from the blood is still in me–I can still smell it. The sound of Matt's heart pumping pounds through my head–I can hear the blood passing through each chamber.

Picturing our wedding and our daughter I fight the temptation as Matt comes closer.

"Hey there baby, how is your training going?"

I try to meditate in order to relax as he gets even closer. I raise my hand, signaling for him to stop, and see Alexander reach out his arm, preventing Matt from getting closer.

"She's doing great, but you have to watch her closely. Make sure you react based only on her signals, and no quick movements. We're all here to ensure your safety," Alexander explains.

"Ebony, can I come say hello and maybe give you a kiss?' Matt questions.

I nod. "Yeah, I'm okay. How was your day?

"Better now that I get to come home to my girls. So how can I help with training?" He moves very cautiously.

"You're helping just by being here." I smile, and stand for a kiss. Everyone's eyes are glued to us, waiting to ensure I can handle the close contact.

# CHAPTER TWENTY-THREE
## Another Milestone

Graduation is finally here. Elijah says I'm ready to go. Only one month after becoming a *vampire*, I'm ready to go out in public. We can only guess that I'm progressing so fast because of my magickal powers. I'm really getting used to the new me, and am so glad that Eliza and Matt don't care or treat me differently. I know Grams, Mom, and Dad were all a little shocked, but they took it better than I expected them to. Being a *vampire* has halted my magick training; I just hope to resume soon, and am more determined than ever to get rid of Naberius. We wanted to banish him in my second trimester, but so much was going on and time just flew by. I'm glad he hasn't made an attempt on us or Elyn, but we do have to deal with him soon. But for now, I need to get ready for grad.

"Sophia, you look beautiful!"

"Thanks Ebony, are you almost ready?"

"Yeah, just gotta put on my dress."

"I'm so proud of you–with everything you've been through this year, you are still graduating at the top of our class."

"It hasn't been easy, but I've had great friends and family to help me."

"And you always will." Sophia gives me a hug.

"So, is Nathanial ready for his valedictorian speech?" I ask.

"Yeah I think so. He refuses to let me hear it."

"Okay, ready. Commencement here we come. How many is this for you now?"

"I don't know, a few dozen maybe, at least for high school. I think you may have to find a spell to age us a few years. Then at least we can get jobs and go to the bars and such," Sophia suggests.

"Yeah–I am sick of high school and this is my first time. I don't know if I could make it through again."

We meet everyone else downstairs, where they are having a celebratory drink. Everyone is here; the Pierce family, the Triggs family–well at least Eliza, since she is the only one left–the McCord family, and of course the Barton family. They are all here to help us celebrate all our achievements. It's nice that the Barton's haven't questioned Matt and me about living at the Pierce house since we had Elyn. They must just assume we wanted to be here close to our friends and with lots of help. I think that one day they may need to know the truth.

In her motherly tone Florence asks, "Are you kids ready? Don't forget your caps and gowns."

"They're already in the car," Sophia answers.

"We should probably go. We don't want to be late; this is too big of a day," Florence adds.

♦ ♦ ♦

The entire graduating class is waiting to be seated in the fold up chairs placed on the football field. Facing the stage we all wait patiently for the dignitaries to enter and the ceremony to begin. Within moments our class leader walks in and the dignitaries all follow. She raises the ceremony baton and pounds the end of it to the ground, signifying the beginning of commencement. We all take our seats as the principal begins his speech. I wish we could all sit together, but because everyone is seated in alphabetical order, Barton is nowhere near Pierce. At least I get to sit next to my wonderful husband, and Alexander has connected our little group telepathically. He wants to make sure they can all keep an eye on me, being my first time in public since my Embrace. Everyone at school thinks it has been because of recovery from Elyn. Sophia has been bringing my work home so I have been able to keep up with the curriculum, allowing me to graduate with my class today. The other reason to link our minds is so we can chat freely, but Matt and I are both so interested in the ceremony that we pay little attention to the others.

Nathanial steps to the podium. "It is great to stand here before you and see the faces of those I grew up with over the years. We have spent the past four years here, and for many of us it has become like a second home and a second family. We have shared in many great memories and many failures together, but today we are here to celebrate the end of a very important stage. Many

183

of us walked through the doors of grade school together and others joined us at different stages of their lives. We have grown together and now the time has come to find the exit and to go out on our own and begin our new lives, as adults." He pauses momentarily and glances around at all the faces we have become accustomed too. "Today we celebrate our achievements. We have made it through both some of the hardest and best years of our lives. Now that exams are finished, our lockers are cleaned out and today we celebrate our accomplishments, we have reached the end of this journey and prepare for a new one: adulthood."

Nathanial continues with a wonderful speech for the next several minutes, after which they begin to call our names to receive our diplomas. One by one we file across the stage and pause for pictures. The end of the ceremony comes quickly and we jump up, throwing our graduation caps into the air, screaming and hugging those around us. This truly has been an amazing experience, and I'm so glad that with everything going on I have been able to participate. We go join our families as they congratulate every one of us.

"We are so proud of each and every one of you. This is a great accomplishment, and we have some surprises for you once we get back to the house," Florence says.

Mrs. Barton cries as she hugs Matt, "I can't believe that my baby has graduated. You really are a man now Matt. Things might have been done a little backwards for you, but the fact that you still got it all done amazes me. I have to admit that when you and

Ebony told us that you were going to have a baby and getting married, I was scared that that would be the end of your education. I can't tell you how proud I am of both of you for following through and completing high school, and I'm even more proud that you both plan on attending college next year. Elyn is a very lucky little girl to have such dedicated and intelligent parents. We love both of you and that beautiful little daughter of yours very much."

"Thanks Mom, I think we're just a little scared. But with such great family and some amazing friends helping us, failure just isn't an option. Plus I think that since things worked out alright for you and Dad doing it all so young, we have great role models to guide us," Matt admits.

Once we share our well wishes with the other students, we decide it is time to head back to the Pierce house for celebrations of our own.

"Do you think we can stop at the manor? I would like to check on things and even pick up some items," I request.

"Sure. Does anyone else want to join us?" Matt asks.

Eliza, Sophia, and Nathanial all agree to escort us to the manor. Everyone else decides to meet us at the house when we're finished.

"We'll take Elyn back to the Pierce house with us," Mrs. Barton offers.

"Thanks Mom," I say. I love calling her mom, although it is still a little awkward. I've never had anyone to call mom while I was growing up and now I have three; my mom, Matt's mom and Florence. I've got such a great life now, and can't wait to see what the future will bring.

◆ ◆ ◆

Arriving at the manor I feel emotional, sad that Elyn isn't getting the chance to grow up in the same home as I did. Entering the front door I sense that something is different.

"Do you feel that Eliza?" I ask.

She gives me an awkward look. "Feel what? I think you are just emotional since it has been so long since you've been here."

"Maybe you're right," I agree as we enter and close the door.

I quickly go up to my room and begin to collect items I want to have with me. As I'm in my room I get a sense that something isn't right again, so I hurry to gather what I need and want, and head back down stairs. In the kitchen I begin to go through our apothecary cabinet to gather supplies we made need to continue our training. I can hear Eliza still upstairs in her room.

Sophia comes into the kitchen. "How you holding up?"

"Not bad–I just have the weirdest feeling being here. It is making me rather uneasy."

I hear a small crash from upstairs and I race to the top floor with all my speed. I shout to Sophia, "Stay with the boys!"

Reaching the top step I hear Eliza cry out for help. I fling her bedroom door open with my telekinetic power and race in. For a moment I pause in shock;, it is him the one we have waited for all this time. Naberius stood nearly seven feet tall, with pale green, scale-like skin, long pointy nose, and chin and eyes as red as blood. I can't believe he is here. The horns protruding from his forehead create a cracked skin effect where they once hid. I still have some of the potions from downstairs in my hands and throw the freezing potion at him. Eliza is on the ground and injured. I can smell her blood and begin to feel the effects. My eyes and throat start to burn, my jaw aches as my fangs begin to protrude. I can't fight the response right now; I have too much adrenaline. I run to Eliza and toss the healing potion; I can see the shock on her face from the change in my appearance. The fangs and black eyes, along with the paling of my skin and dark circles under my eyes, is something my sister hasn't seen yet.

"It's okay sis; it is still me! It's just the blood and adrenaline causing it. Now let's get this bastard!"

She smiles and points behind me. Naberius is fighting the effects of the freezing potion, and is headed towards us. Deciding to use my newly acquired vampire skills I lunge at him; he is surprised by my speed and strength.

"I took your parents; *witches*, and I will take you as well," he growls.

With me physically fighting him Eliza gets the chance to recover and get the potions I have organized.

"We'll defeat you," I swear. "You had no right to take our parents."

Eliza jumps to her feet and I see Sophia in the door holding more supplies.

"I thought I said stay with the boys!" I scream.

He hits Eliza with a fireball. I think to myself, *I can't look. Sophia is there she'll help her. I need to continue the fight.*

"I got her Ebony—don't worry, she'll be fine," Sophia yells.

"Kay, so what about the boys?" I yell while emerged in hand-to-hand battle with the demon.

"Alexander's here, he was still connected to us when we got here and heard everything. He came right over. So he is taking the boy's home and I can help," she explains.

Eliza sits up to check through the supplies Sophia brought up from the apothecary cabinet. "I'm good; let me see what we got here."

I continue to fight, gnawing and slashing at the demon, trying to remember the moves Isaac taught me. I'm faster and physically stronger, but he is taking everything I can dish out to him. I can tell he is growing tired of this physical fight, as I am overpowering him. He pushes me back with all his might and holds me back with some kind of mental force field.

"I can't get to him anymore," I exclaim.

Eliza and Sophia come to my side. Eliza throws a protection potion at our feet and then a power-weakening vial at Naberius' feet. I can feel his connection holding me, but it's not as strong. He feels it too, and releases only to throw a type of electrical current at us.

"Move!" Sophia shouts and pushes us down, forgetting about the protection spell. I flip up to my feet and toss a reversing potion; anything he tries to do to us should be mirrored back at him.

"He's too strong for the potions we need to banish him; do you remember the spell?" I ask Eliza.

"I do, do you?" she replies.

Nodding, we hold hands and begin to chant.

> "By the power in we,
> We banish thee,
> He who took what belonged,
> Release in time,
> And be gone.
> By the power in we,
> We banish thee.
> So mote it be,
> So mote it be,
> So mote it be."

The three of us stand and watch as a black hole reaching deeper than the pits of hell opens before us. Naberius then implodes and the particles are sucked into the pit, swirling like a tornado. The force exuded from him throws us against the far wall with more force than I have ever felt. Eliza and I hold one another and with tears of joy we cry together. We did it; we got rid of the demon that took Mom and Dad from us.

CHARLOTTE BLACKWELL

# CHAPTER TWENTY-FOUR
## Celebrations

Back at the Pierce house we need to be careful about what we discuss. Nathanial's family the McCords, and the Bartons, are still unaware about our supernatural natures. We can celebrate defeating Naberius later; now is time to celebrate our graduation. Eliza and I take our belongings up to our rooms and clean up a little before anyone else can notice. I can hear Elyn crying downstairs and hurry to her.

"Hey baby girl, Mommy's here. What's the matter?" I give her a little kiss on the head and she clasps onto me tightly.

Mrs. McCord comes to my side, "I have never seen a baby so young clutch on to someone in that way before. It is almost as though she's scared."

"I don't know what is wrong; she has never done this before." I explain, "I think I'll take her into the library for a few moments. Maybe all the excitement and people from graduation is too much for her."

"I will bring a bottle for her," Alexander offers.

"Thanks Alexander," I say as I go around the corner to the library. I know that his offer is because he wants to talk to me about something. I hope he can explain what is going on with Elyn–she's never acted like this before.

I love the Pierce's library; it is so relaxing in here. Sitting in the soft leather rocker/glider I get Elyn's favorite book 'Goodnight Moon'; it always seems to calm her. Moments later Alexander walks in with her bottle.

"So what's up Alexander?" I ask, taking the bottle and feeding Elyn.

"As you already know I can't get full thoughts from Elyn; since she is just a baby the thought process is not developed enough."

"Yeah, but you must be getting something."

"I did; she was genuinely terrified that she was going to lose you. I think her powers go far beyond levitation. I think she has premonitions of some sort. Maybe she can see what you are doing. She knew you were in a big fight today. I don't know how, but I get that sense from her," he explains.

"So how do we figure this out?"

"Well I was thinking I could hold her, or even just her hand, and try to focus all my telepathic power to her. Maybe that way I can get a better picture of what she's experiencing."

"It's worth a try," I agree.

Alexander decides to sit next to Elyn and try to hold her hand. He closes his eyes and concentrates, before long I see his eyes moving very quickly behind his closed lids, almost like R.E.M. He has a panicked expression on his face. My concern grows as I have never seen Alexander get panicked about anything before. Wanting to ask what is going on; I resist the urge, as I don't want to disrupt him. Suddenly his eyes pop wide open and he glances down at Elyn then back to me.

"This poor little thing," Alexander announces.

I grow frantic, "What? What's the matter?"

"She is not having premonitions–she is full on experiencing the fear and pain of those she loves. She's an empathy–Elyn feels the fear and pain you experienced while fighting Naberius."

"But I didn't feel any pain," I insist.

"You may not realize it since you are a *vampire* now or because of the adrenaline rush you had. You still feel pain, physical as well as emotional. Elyn sensed your emotional pain when Eliza was injured, and from fighting the demon that killed your parents. She also sensed your physical pain from the fight with him. Being so young, she does not understand that your pain was only temporary and she was scared for you. In time she will learn to deal with this power better."

I look down at the beautiful little girl in my arms. "I'm alright, Peanut. You don't need to worry about Mommy. It is my job to worry about you." I turn my attention to Alexander. "So why is she getting multiple powers at such a young age?"

"That I don't know–you may have to contact your ancestors about this. Maybe there is a way to help her control it. From my understanding children do show signs of their powers, but it's not supposed to be so strong," he answers.

Now that Elyn is calm again, we rejoin the celebration. Matt's mom comes right over to Elyn and me. She is a wonderful grandmother.

"There's my beautiful little grandbaby. Wanna come see Grandma?" She reaches out for Elyn. "Are you happier now?"

"She is, and she always loves her time with you." I smile as I carefully pass Elyn over with a light hand on the back of her head for support.

Everyone is relaxing and enjoying time together. The Barton's, McCord's, Pierce's and Eliza all give out graduation gifts to us. This is so exciting—how did I ever get so lucky to be surrounded by so many wonderful people? It wasn't that long ago that I felt so alone and on my own, but now I know I never have to worry about feeling that way again. My life is beyond complete and I couldn't be happier.

Mrs. McCord begins to cling her glass. "I would like to say a few words."

Everyone in the room quiets down and we all turn our attention to her.

"Today our youngest has completed a huge step forward, and with so many great friends at his side. You've all become like family to us, and we can only pray that it stays this way. Nate, your father and I are so proud of you for receiving a full scholarship to Harvard. We are just as proud of the rest of you for your accomplishments as well. Now, with both our boys attending college, we should be preparing for our freedom." She smiles.

"Gee thanks Mom." Nathanial jokes.

"You know what I mean, kid. Anyways, as you all know, Arthur and I have wanted another baby for a long time, and yet we gave up years ago. The doctors always maintain that we could not conceive or reverse the damage. I went for my regular check up a few weeks ago and they found out something interesting," she continues.

"Mom, are you going to be okay?" Luke asks.

Mr. McCord goes to his sons, "Your mother is fine. There is nothing to worry about. Let her finish and you'll see."

"Okay, well the doctor ran some regular tests and that lead to some diagnostic imaging. It turns out that all the damage has repaired itself. And I'm now expecting," she announces with a smile.

"Oh my god Mom, Dad, this is amazing!" Luke jumps to his feet and hugs his parents.

We all jump and scream, and I notice Nathanial give Sophia a little wink. I can't believe she did it— Sophia healed Nathanial's mom, without her knowledge.

Florence brings out some sparkling cider. "Nikole and Arthur, we wish you and your new baby all the best. You too have become like family to us. Little Elyn has brought such joy to our close group and I think it is safe to say that we are all excited to welcome another little one."

As the group celebrates, I take Matt off to the side. I want to make sure he is okay from everything that happened at the manor. We are only gone for a few

195

moments; Matt insists he is fine and we both agree that that fight is over with. Naberius can no longer captivate mine and Eliza's thoughts, and to think we actually graduated. This has been such an incredible day, what could possibly happen next?

# CHAPTER TWENTY-FIVE
## Moving

School finishes and summer is finally here; things have been extremely quiet and normal the past few weeks. Now that school is officially over we can enjoy our summer. Luke's returning from school this week and will be moving into the manor with Eliza. They have such an amazing connection I know they belong together. We continue to pack Eliza's belongings to go back home. Elijah and Florence come upstairs to take the next load down.

"Are you sure that you will be alright at the manor, by yourself?" Florence's motherly concern comes out.

"I won't be alone; Luke will be with me."

"I mean, without any other powers or help."

"Florence, I love you all, but I can't stay here forever. Luke and I are going to try things out over the summer, see how they work. Also, Ebony is going to come with me and we will use the great mystical power to put a protection on the manor." Eliza hugs Florence, the woman who has been like a mother to us since the day we lost Grams.

"I love you girls too, that is why I worry."

Elijah steps forward. "Are you ladies done with all this sappy stuff yet?"

"Yes dear." Florence nudges.

"Now, Ebony and Matt, since Eliza is going back to the manor, and Ebony you have proven yourself, Florence and I decided that as a new family, your two and your little peanut deserve some privacy. We had the guesthouse out back fixed up. Everything is in full working condition and we stocked the fridge and cupboards for you Matt," Elijah explains.

I look at Matt and then Florence and Elijah, in shock and unable to conceal my excitement. "Oh my god, are you kidding me? We get our very own place, like a real married couple?"

Elijah chuckles, "Well for all intents and purposes, yes. We are still close by and a tunnel connects the main house to the guesthouse. Alex will be checking in on you every so often, and we expect you, Ebony, every night for dinner. You too are welcome Matt. Florence can have something prepared for you as well. We just want to make sure that Ebony remains well fed."

"I think those are very agreeable terms," I squeal, not able to control my excitement.

Matt smiles and grabs me around the waist and swings me. "Of course, I agree to those terms."

"It's settled then. Once we get Eliza moved back into the manor we will move you over to the guest house," Florence says as she grabs another basket of Eliza's clothes.

♦ ♦ ♦

At the manor, after we unload the cars, Eliza and I place a magnificent protection spell on the manor. This is our way of ensuring that nothing supernatural can attack Eliza, Luke, or anyone else for that matter, while they are here.

"Ebony, I was thinking that you should keep the Book of Shadows. You have far more time to learn from it and study than I do," Eliza acknowledges.

"Are you sure? I do enjoy reading it when Elyn and Matt are asleep."

"I'm sure. It is not like we're never going to see each other."

It doesn't take long to get her set up and comfortable.

"Will you be okay for a few days until Luke gets here?" I ask as I hug my big sister.

"I will be—I'm just so excited and can't wait for him to get here."

"You can't wait for whom to get here?" a husky voice asks from the doorway.

"Luke! What are you doing here? I thought you would be a few more days." Eliza exudes excitement as she runs into his arms.

The rest of us take that as our cue to leave, saying a quick goodbye, and then we sneak out the door.

◆ ◆ ◆

"Can you believe Luke came to surprise her that way? He is so amazing," I gush.

We all giggle as we head back to the house, and then my cell phone rings.

"Hello?"

"Hi, Ebony?" A male voice asks.

"Yes."

"I'm sorry to call you out of the blue, this is Dakota Williams."

"Hi Dakota, it is nice to hear from you. How's your family doing?"

"Everyone is good. I'm sorry we have not been in touch more. There has been some activity in the area and we have been tracking it. I didn't want to involve any of you until I knew for sure," he starts.

"What do you mean—what is it you have been tracking?" I enquire.

"There are more vampires in the area. I recognize one of them from last time."

"That's impossible, we destroyed them all," I argue."Are you sure they are not new ones up from Boston?"

"I'm sure, I suspect that one of them escaped or was left behind," Dakota reasons.

"Okay, have your family meet us at the Peirce house tonight and we'll discuss what you know."

I begin to inform Elijah and Florence about Dakota, but they heard everything while Dakota and I were speaking. I give Matt a brief run down on the way back to the house.

"I guess we will not be relocating to the guest house tonight," he pouts.

"Matt you are living with a family of super fast, super strong *vampires*. I'm assuming that Alex, Mati and Sophia already have your stuff moved," Florence smirks.

"Your family is too much. One day my powers will kick in too, you know."

I smack him on the arm, "Don't you dare! If your powers 'kick in' you're dead and you have a wife and daughter that need you."

"Fine, fine, I will leave the powers to you." He leans over and kisses me as the car pulls up to the house.

♦ ♦ ♦

Walking in the front door and looking around the house we have lived in for the past few months, I can't help but smile. The grand staircase, the dining room that Florence serves every gourmet blood meal in, and the family room where it all happens, I know we won't be far but I will miss this house.

Sophia runs in all excited, "We got it all done, your new house is ready and Elyn is already napping in her nursery! Mati is there with her."

"Can we see it?" I ask enthusiastically.

"Of course, let's take the tunnel." Sophia grabs our hands to lead the way.

We have never seen or used the tunnel before; now that I think of it I have never even seen the guest house. Under the grand staircase in the hidden room, Sophia pushes on another door that takes us down a long tunnel. As we walk the lights ahead of us brighten to light our way; they must be on motion sensors. I examine the walls as we walk further into the tunnel, "What are all these pictures on the walls?" I ask.

Florence, Elijah and Sophia all smile and look at one another. Elijah explains, "These are our portraits from over the years. We keep them here for our personal recollection, without allowing others who come into our home to see. If anyone saw some of these, questions would arise that we're not prepared to answer."

"I really want to hear about some of these, but another time. I want to see our new home."

"Well it is not much further, just that panel up ahead." Sophia giggles as she spins around to face me.

She pushes open the panel and leads us into the most beautiful little bungalow. I practically freeze in the spot, looking around. I think someone stole one of my wish books; this looks just like the room I designed. White leather couches, a rock wall fireplace, a natural wood dinner table and every piece of baby furniture a person could imagine.

"This is amazing!" I turn and examine every corner, and every little decorative piece.

"This is just like your books," Matt announces.

Alexander steps forward, "Yeah, so one cool thing about telepathy is no one can hide anything from you."

Sophia gives Matt and I the tour; the place is amazing. There's not an inch of wasted space, little niche's and cubby's everywhere. We enter Elyn's nursery, a larger room with a round crib in the center of the room. A small circle hangs from the ceiling with beautiful white satin and pink tulle hanging from it, draping around the crib. Two small bookshelves sit on the other side of the room, one filled with wonderful children's books, the other with toys and stuffed animals. A rocker, a change table and dresser—everything is fully stocked. They painted her room with a life size mural, one side is the sun and nature, the other is the moon and stars. We leave Elyn to rest in her new room; she looks so peaceful.

The doorbell rings from the main house; Sophia looks puzzled, "Who could that be?"

"Oh, I didn't tell you. Dakota called; there's a problem. The Williams are coming by to discuss what they know," I inform.

"We better get back to the house. Grab the baby monitor," Sophia suggests.

"It's okay, I'll stay here with Elyn. I'm no help over there anyways. Elyn and I can hang out here together," Matt insists.

The rest of us run back through the tunnel returning to the main house in only seconds.

"Hey there Dakota, it's been a long time," Alexander says as he opens the door.

CHARLOTTE BLACKWELL

# CHAPTER TWENTY-SIX
## Surprise Guests

It's been about eighteen months since this group of supernatural beings was all in the same room together. It doesn't take long for Eliza and Luke to arrive. Luke and Nathanial both join Matt in the guesthouse so not to disturb the rest of us. Florence, Elijah, Isaac, Constance, Alexander, Matilda, Sophia, and Danika are all present. Eliza, along with Dakota and Tamo Williams, and myself are ready to discuss the issue at hand.

"Where is everyone else from your tribe?" Alexander asks.

"Dad and I thought it would be best for the rest of the *shape shifters* to continue patrolling the area," Dakota explains.

"So what's been happening that has you concerned?" Matilda questions.

Tamo stands and begins to walk the room, "We have noticed a familiar face in recent weeks. One of the Cerberus vampires from before has returned. He is stronger and has built another army."

"I don't understand—we destroyed them. Decapitation, burning their remains and burying the ashes in various silver boxes ensured they could not regenerate." Danika recaps, then her facial expression falls. "Do you think it's Drake?"

"Not sure who Drake is, but we do recognize this one. The only thing that we can figure is he was hiding during the fight," Dakota admits.

"Drake is the new leader of all the Cerberus; he tried to make Danika his queen," Alexander adds.

We go over the details that the shifters have collected and all agree that we need to plan another attack. Since Eliza and I have become so strong, our powers will be a bigger help than last time. The sound of footsteps start to come up the front porch, and we all turn to Alexander for confirmation.

"It's okay; you may find something interesting behind the door." Alexander smiles, as he walks to the front foyer.

We all follow as Elijah goes to the door. After just one slight knock Elijah swings open the door, and before him stands a surprise.

"Caspian!" Sophia runs to the arms of her estranged brother.

"Well I must say; this is quite the pleasant surprise." Elijah says as he hugs the man that he has always thought of as a son.

"It is nice to see you all again," the tall man forever locked in his early twenties replies.

"To what do we owe this pleasure? I thought the Cerberus from Boston had you on a short leash," Isaac wonders.

"Yeah they do, but I felt this was important enough to make contact," he says as he flips his long black hair out of his face.

After saving Danika earlier this year from club VC, Caspian returned and begged for forgiveness. He was tortured for thirty days before joining them. However, joining them is only a ruse he is using to gather information for us. The cult still has their doubts about him, so it makes it difficult for him to contact us.

Sophia is giddy with excitement, "Does this mean you are back to stay?"

"Let's just take things one step at a time."

"So what's up Caspian? We haven't seen much of you since we rescued Danika from Club VC. Is something happening, do you have news for us?" Alexander asks, even though he probably knows already.

We return to the family room and get comfortable. Florence and Constance bring in beverages for everyone. Caspian is intent on sharing something with us.

"So as much as I would love to catch up, I have something pressing to discuss. I promise to fill you in on everything later," Caspian insists.

"Then what is it?" I ask.

"Okay, wait a second;, have I missed something or are you a *vampire* now Ebony?"

We all chuckle. "Yeah, long story but you are stuck with me now. Oh yeah, by the way, you're an uncle."

"Okay, we are going to need to catch up on some family stuff soon too. Let's get business out of the way in case I have to get outta here fast. So I guess you're already clued in, considering the gather of supernatural beings in this room."

"We came to warn your family about one of the Cerberus that we originally fought. He is in the area and has rebuilt an army," Tamo announces.

"That is exactly why I am here too. I have been undercover with them as one of the leader's militant's. This way I can try to learn his plan and relay the information back to you."

"I still do not think this is the safest plan," Florence shows her concern.

Caspian takes hold of Florence's hand, "I have been in and around the underground scene for many years now. I have tried to remain under the radar, that is until the stuff with Danika. I don't want you to worry—they are beginning to trust my intentions again."

"How do you know I'm a *vampire* now?" I ask, still stuck on the previous conversation.

"I guess you don't know." Caspian chuckles and glances at his estranged family. "You are well aware of everyone's powers, have they ever told you what my power is?"

"No, I don't ask too many questions about you, because I know how painful it was for them to lose you," I admit.

"Well Ebony, I'm able to sense others of supernatural descent."

"So that is how you know I'm a *vampire*; you can tell what kind of supernatural others are too?" I confirm.

"You got it–pretty cool, huh."

"I'd say. That'd sure come in handy for me and Eliza."

The next few hours are spent comparing notes between the Williams and Caspian. It appears as though we might have another big fight on our hands. I wonder if I should tell the others about the dreams I started having recently. They've been so vivid and life like, I'm not sure what to make of them. I gotta remember it's just a dream. Maybe I will do some research on dream interpretation, and I think it is time to contact Grams again soon.

"Ebony, are you okay? You seem lost in space." Danika kneels before me.

"Yeah everything is fine, just thinking." I glance over at Alexander, asking him not to say anything.

◆ ◆ ◆

After everyone leaves, Alexander, Eliza and Sophia escort me through the tunnel toward the guest house. Alexander telepathically asks me if it is okay to talk about it now, and I agree.

"So tell me about these dreams Ebony," he requests.

"Well, I know it was just a dream but it seems so realistic," I start to explain.

"What about your dream is so realistic?" Sophia asks.

"In my dreams since my Embrace, I have seen and talked to *ghosts*, and various types of *angels*."

Everyone stops in their tracks for moment, pondering the possibilities of what I've been seeing.

"Why don't you tell us a little more about the *ghosts* you've been seeing?" Eliza suggests.

"Like I said I know it's a dream, and I'm not actually seeing them."

"That's the thing Ebony, now that you are a *vampire*, you don't require much rest. You do tend to get more than the average new *vampire*, because of the fulfillment in your life, but nonetheless. Well, what I'm trying to say is, basically, *vampires* don't dream. We don't go into deep enough sleep to enter the dream state. So, you might just be resting and whatever you are seeing appears to be a dream, when it just might be reality," Alexander explains.

Alexander's explanation concerns me a little. Could the ability to see *ghosts* be a new power for me? Could it be possible that I'm a medium? It would only make sense that since my Embrace my powers would increase, since all my other senses increased. From what I've learned too, it's normal for powers that the mortal wasn't aware of, to appear once Embraced. "So what happens when these *ghosts* come to you?" Eliza inquires.

"Nothing really special–I don't feel any threat or danger from them. I think they just want my help, like they're lost souls looking for their way home. They seem to be very aware of the supernatural. They talk about demons, and have even mentioned about me being a *witch*."

"I think that may be a logical explanation being that you and your sister are the Magnificent Ones. They could be coming to you for help; it sounds as though they may have been killed by *demons* and need your help to move on into the light," Sophia suggests.

"And what about the *Angels*–could they be more like *guardians*? Maybe Matt should tell his instructors about what is happening, and they may know. I guess I should tell him about the dreams," I ponder.

"I have to say I'm surprised you haven't talked to him about this already," Eliza says with complete shock.

# CHARLOTTE BLACKWELL

# CHAPTER TWENTY-SEVEN
## Understanding

Sitting down with the boys, we begin to fill them in on the information from our meeting with the Williams family. Nathanial can tell that Sophia's been extremely emotional. We explain about Caspian returning. He instantly takes Sophia into his arms, knowing how much her estranged brother means to her, and how she must feel having him back at the house after he left again to pledge to the Cerberus.

"Are you okay sweetie?" He asks.

She leans her head on his shoulder, "I am, and can't believe that he's back, it's been months. I hate that he has to pretend to be in with those idiots at club VC. I just hope that he stays. I don't think I can handle losing him again"

Alexander stands and begins to pace the room; we all know this is a sign. He begins his lecture, "Well I don't think that we can pressure him, but I think it is important that he knows how much he's been missed over the years. When he helped us save Danika, he was insistent that he needed to be away, to go back to the Cerberus to help the family better. Now that it appears that the Cerberus is ready to make a move again, maybe he'll be ready to rejoin the family."

"I guess we can only hope," Sophia adds.

I begin to get a feeling of déjà vu, as we talk about the Cerberus returning. I anticipate that we can be as lucky as last time ensuring that no one from Wenham gets hurt. We enlighten the boys as to all the information Tamo and Dakota shared with us as well as well, as the Intel Caspian has been collecting.

"When we destroyed the Cerberus before, we assumed we had the leader of that group. It turns out he was second in command and the leader was hiding far enough away that none of us knew. As you know there's always more of them and Drake is now the leader since his rise to ascension. Caspian confirmed that Drake, formally known as Drako is the creation of Cyrus, one of the original thirteen grandchildren of Cain," Sophia explains.

"And what does it mean that he is one of the great-grandchildren?" Luke asks.

"Well, it's a long story Luke, but the short version is Cain was cursed by God and made the first *vampire*. Because he was lonely, he created more and then they created more, which brings us to the original thirteen grandchildren. Like most siblings they began to fight and took sides. Some of them became the Renata, which is the group that enforces the vampiric laws. The remainder of them became the Cerberus. If Drake is a descendent of one of the original grandchildren, he could be centuries old and extremely powerful." Alexander gives a quick explanation.

"And you are expected to fight one of the oldest living *vampires* in history? Are you all freakin crazy?" Luke jumps to his feet in protest.

"Luke hon, you have to remember that Ebony and I are two of the most powerful *witches* the world has ever seen. And the Pierce family has worked with the Renata in the past, and been successful." Eliza stands to face Luke, holding his hands as she explains.

"You and your sister may be the most powerful *witches*, but you are new *witches* and still learning your craft," Matt disputes. "Not to mention she's my wife and mother to my daughter."

"Well I guess we're just going to have to work a little harder at learning more about magick," she insists.

Elyn begins to cry from the other room. I chuckle as everyone in the room jumps to go get her. As I walk towards the room I wave them all back to their seats. I soon return with Elyn, and place the swing next to Matt.

"So there's something else that has been happening," I say, lowering my head.

"What is it, Ebony? You know, you can tell me anything." Matt takes hold of my hand.

"Well, I thought I was having dreams about *ghosts* and *Angels*, until Alexander explained that *vampires* don't enter a dream state, and that the *ghosts* are probably approaching me. I don't want you to worry and feel threatened by them; I think they need my help. But I am hoping that you can help me with the *angel* part."

"I'll help you with anything that I can. What do you need me to do?"

"What do you know about *angels*? I'm wondering if these could actually be our *guardians*. We've known that we are *witches* for most two years now and we still have never seen any sign of our *guardian* yet. Now I know you said he or she will come to us when we need it most."

Matt goes to get some of his training books and begins to look through the pages as if he knows what to look for.

"What is it you're looking for Matt?" I ask sitting down next to him.

"I just remember learning about *angels*. They don't usually show themselves or make their presence known. There's got to be a reason that they've came to you," Matt explains as he continues to search his notes.

"What would an *angel* possibly want with a *vampire witch*?" Eliza asks.

"From what I can find in my notes *angels* appear to those that can help them. They must believe that you are able to help them with something. Now we just have to figure out what it is they need help with." Matt closes his books and puts them on the table.

I decide it's a good idea to put all our concerns aside and enjoy the rest of the night with friends. Eliza and I can try to contact Grams later.

"So Nate, how's your mom feeling, and how far along she anyways?" I ask.

"She is actually feeling pretty good. She's getting huge." He laughs, "Turns out she is due the middle of

November. Mom and Dad wanted to wait until they were sure that Mom wouldn't miscarry. She's like five or six months now; to be honest I don't really pay much attention. I'm happy for them, but come on–I'm a guy, how excited can I get?" he jokes.

Sophia gives him a little slap. I think it's so funny, how she tries to keep him in line. Yet amazing how less than two years ago, I felt like such an outsider. Matt and I had just started dating when I received my powers. I didn't think anyone could accept me and I tried to push him away. When Sophia showed up I was terrified that everything was going to go down the toilet. Looking around the room at those who mean so much to me, I'm flabbergasted at how things have changed. and how I've not only grown to love them as friends but as family too. I would've never thought of myself as lucky before, but how can I not. When I see my wonderful husband, our daughter, my sister and her true love, and my two best friends all around me, I feel completely blessed.

"I think we all better go and let the three of you enjoy your first night here," Alexander suggests.

"Thank you so much for trying to help me figure all this out. I guess we'll have to try and come up with another plan to fight the Cerberus again."

As the others see their way out Matt and I get ready for a nice cozy night on the couch with some movies on.

"So now that the others are gone, can we try to figure out what these *angels* may want from me?" I ask while pulling my knees close to my chest and turning to look at Matt.

"I've been trying to remember my lessons, and all I can really say are *angels* are complicated."

"What do you mean?"

"There are many different kinds of *angels*. There are *guardian angels, arc angels, fallen angels* and even something called *nephilim*."

"A *nephilim*; what the hell is a *nephilim*?"

"A *nephilim* is the offspring of an *angel*, most commonly a *fallen angel* and a mortal. They appear to be mortal, until their eighteenth birthday. At which point, they began to gain powers."

"What kind of powers, do they get?"

Matt takes a deep breath, "Well, that is where things get really complicated. They get their wings, for one, which gives them the power to fly. They also gain all the powers that *angels* have. Now sometimes this is good, but just like anything else a *nephilim* can be good or bad," he tries to explain.

"So you're telling me there are people walking around with wings under their coat?"

"Not quite; their wings are concealed unless they need them. They can have white, black, grey or even a combination of these colors in their wings. The purest of *angels* have white wings; over time evil can turn them grey or black. Just don't assume that white is safe; if the *angel* just turned to serve evil their wings may not have changed yet. *Nephilim* and these kind of *angels* are very different from guardians and the Great Ones–they are very secretive so we have minimal knowledge about them."

I crawl up next to Matt and rest my head on his shoulder, trying to ponder what the *angels* could want from me, and how I'm going to help them. My mind is starting to work overtime, wondering why all these supernatural beings are coming to me. I guess I'm just going to have to wait for them to come to me again.

# CHAPTER TWENTY-EIGHT
## Dinner Plans

The Cerberus hasn't attacked as quickly as last time; this concerns me. Although we have more time to train I worry about what they're up to. With everything going on, all of us from the group that graduated decide to put off college for a year with the exception of Nathanial; since he's receiving a scholarship there is no choice but for him to go. I know that Sophia feels he's safer at Harvard with Luke. I also know it's hard for him to leave with his mom having the baby in only two months. Sophia plans to drive up to visit him quite often; he also drives home on the weekends when he and Luke aren't training. It's only been three weeks since he's been gone, but at least we don't have to be concerned about him when the Cerberus attacks again.

As I walk into the manor, Eliza comes running and throws her arms around me.

"Hey, you okay sis?" I ask.

"Yeah I am great; I just miss having you around. Plus I miss my beautiful little niece." She winks as she grab Elyn's carrier from me. "Come on Elyn, let's get you out of the seat." Eliza takes Elyn to the family room and begins to unbuckle the harness straps.

"Um….oh never mind," I prepare to warn Eliza, but chuckle at the thought of letting her see for herself.

She gets the straps off Elyn's shoulders and prepares to lift her from the seat. "Come here, aunties little peanut."

Elyn reaches her arms up and floats right out of her carrier, circling Eliza. I can't help but burst into laughter watching Eliza's mouth hit the ground as she swings around.

"What the…?" she screams.

"Oh, I guess you haven't played tag with Elyn yet," I say, barely able to get the words out.

Matt walks in, lets out a hearty chuckle and says, "Elyn, stop teasing your auntie and give her a hug."

Elyn smiles and lands right in Eliza's arms. "Your daddy was right when he called you trouble, even before you were born," Eliza kisses her. "So is everyone else on their way?"

"Yeah Sophia and Nate should be here shortly, as well as the rest of the Pierce family. Is Luke here yet?"

"Oh yeah, he is helping me cook dinner. It's nice having him back. I know school has only been back in for a few weeks, but I really miss having him around," Eliza admits.

"Will the McCord's be joining us as well?" Matt asks.

"Of course, I couldn't steal both their sons and not invite them to come for dinner."

Sophia, Nathanial, Alexander and Matilda arrive shortly after us. I can't help but wonder where the rest of the family is. I notice they are all fairly somber.

"What's wrong, where is everyone else?" Eliza questions with concern.

"It is time; the Cerberus are just on the outskirts of town. The rest of the family is setting up a perimeter. The William's have taken their forms and are patrolling, keeping close to the Cerberus. Alexander has an open connection with them, but I think we better gather supplies and go as well," Sophia answers.

"What? Not tonight!" Luke shouts.

"I'm sorry Luke. We have to do this so that the innocent people of Wenham don't get hurt," Matilda apologizes.

"I was hoping to have a nice dinner with all our families. I wanted things to be special" he admits.

I notice Alexander look at Luke with wide eyes, and Luke shakes his head. I can't help but wonder what is going on.

"Luke I think you should continue dinner with your family and Matt. You boys will need to keep an eye on Elyn while we fight. This is the safest place for all of you," I insist. Because of the protection spell we've placed on the manor, this is the safest place in town.

"And what do you suggest I tell my parents when they get here, and none of you are here?"

"Hun, I'm sorry to put you in this situation. You can just tell them we had an emergency. That way you aren't lying to them." Eliza looks devastated putting Luke in this situation.

"Okay, I can't fight it so don't worry about us. You better go get everything you need," Luke hugs Eliza. "And please stay safe. I want you coming home to me."

We go to the closet and collect all the supplies we had packed and prepared. I quickly give Matt and Elyn a kiss. It's hard to leave as Elyn is showing signs of her empathy powers and starts freaking out.

Matt takes her in his arms, "Don't worry about her. I'll calm her. You have to concentrate on the fight."

"We gotta go now! They are in the town and attacking. They caused a car accident on Main Street," Alexander yells, as he grabs a bag. "Mati, you drive Eliza the rest of us will go on foot it will be faster."

♦ ♦ ♦

We run out the door, and head to the scene of the accident.

I can't help but wonder who's been hurt in the accident, and also worry about being revealed to the town people. If this fight is going to take place in the middle of town someone is bound to find out about us. I guess we'll have to deal with the repercussions after. Sophia, Alexander and I arrive at the scene of the accident within minutes. As we arrive a Cerberus *vampire* is feeding off one of the accident victims.

Sophia begins to freak out, "Oh my god! I know that car, it's…" She runs faster towards the car.

Alexander chases after the Cerberus, and I notice once of the *shape shifters* flying above in his eagle form. He swoops down and grabs a satchel of wooden stakes in his claws. Then he disappears into the moonlight. Sophia, Matilda and I race to the car and the victims.

224

Pulling them from the car, I realize it is the McCords. No wonder Sophia is so frantic.

"I have to heal them," she cradles Nathanial's expectant mother in her arms. "NO!" Sophia buries her head in Nikole McCord's chest.

"What is it, why can't you help her?" I ask.

"She's gone. Her life force has left her, you know that once that happens I can't help."

"The baby too?" I gasp.

"Yes...wait...I can sense it. Call Isaac now!" she orders.

Matilda and Eliza arrive, Matilda calls Isaac and he arrives in a blink of an eye, scooping Mrs. McCord into his arms. "I will get her to the hospital and perform an emergency cesarean section, and try to save the baby." He's gone just as fast as he arrived. He is going to have to move at lightning speed to make it on time. Without performing CPR on Mrs. McCord, the blood won't circulate through her body, causing the baby to also die.

"Oh no, what about Nathanial's dad?" I remember.

"I sensed that he was gone the moment we pulled up. He must have died right away. What am I going to tell Nathanial and Luke?" Sophia worries.

"I'm worried about them too, but first we need to roast the assholes that did this." Eliza says with a fire in her eyes I've never seen before.

# CHARLOTTE BLACKWELL

# CHAPTER TWENTY-NINE
## Changes

Rogue *vampires* begin surrounding us; Elijah, Florence, Constance and Danika all arrive, taking out a few by surprise as they join us. There must be at least fifty *vampires* closing in on us. I notice the town's people taking cover, at least the few that were left on the streets. Eliza pulls out the potions from her bag. This is Danika's first fight; she was too new the first time around, but since her experience at Club VC everyone agreed she has matured enough. I guess they figure because of my mystical powers and how well my training is going that I will be alright.

"That one there, he's getting closer." She points and he bounces off a force field.

"What the hell was that?" I ask.

"I have no idea; I guess I am finally getting a new power," Eliza suggests.

"Okay let's use this to our advantage. Try to place a force field around our group," I suggest.

227

The *vampires* come closer; we need to ensure that we can still attack through the shield. Elijah throws a stake aiming at one of the *vampires*; it penetrates the field and stakes one right in the heart.

"Okay, this is good, but we don't have enough stakes," Danika notes.

"And I can't hold this much longer," Eliza admits.

"I have an idea. Elijah, Florence, I need both of you to throw a stake, as hard and fast as you can," I order.

As they each throw a stake I use my telekinetic power to move the stake through as many of the *vampires* as I can. It penetrates through each *vampire* completely moving on to the next one with full force.

"Ebony, you just took out over half of the Cerberus with only two stakes," Danika says with surprise.

We watch as the staked *vampires* turn to dried-up corpses ready to be beheaded and burned. Then Eliza collapses to the ground and the force field retracts. Caspian comes racing in with six shifters right behind him. I pick up the protection potion and throw it down at Eliza, as we run and physically attack the remaining Cerberus. Sophia is out for *vampire* blood. She wants to destroy them for taking her boyfriend's parents. I can't help but think the boys are going to be destroyed. As we fight we all hear a cell phone ringing from the McCord's car. The boy's must be trying to call and find out where their parents are. Alexander connects to Nathanial and tells him to stay at the manor. He explains that the boy's parents are at the hospital with Isaac, and no one can leave. We all look at him, knowing it's not really a lie, but a stretch of the truth that must be told to protect the others.

"Alexander, watch out there's one behind you," Matilda warns as she flips her attacker over right on to a broken tree branch and stakes him.

Elijah is going hard with the fight leader, one of Drake's head hunters. Caspian described him when he came to the house that day, and this must be him. He is powerful and fits the physical description. Just under six feet tall, shoulder length brown curly hair, goatee and black eyes surrounded by a red rim so bright it glows. Elijah narrowly misses a stake in the chest when he turns as the leader moves to pick one up from the ground and nicks his arm. Others try to help their leader as we attempt to keep them clear of Elijah.

Through peripheral vision I see Eliza coming to. "Ebony, catch," she shouts as she throws a trapping potion. I throw it at Elijah, Caspian and the leader, trapping them together so no others can interfere. This gives us an advantage, since no one can help the leader now. Danika gets hurt in her altercation with a female *vampire*. I think it may be the *vampire* named Marcie Danika told us about. I wasn't at the club when they rescued Danika, so I never got a look at any of the *vampires* there.

"Sophia, help," Danika shouts.

Sophia races to her sister's side, as she lies there with broken limbs. Sophia helps her heal faster as Eliza throws a force field around them just long enough to protect them. Elijah and Caspian are finally able to stake the leader and suddenly the other Cerberus weaken enough that we can destroy them easily.

"Now that was easy. Why is it that they were weakened so once the leader was destroyed?" I ask.

Elijah smiles, "Whenever a *vampires* creator is destroyed it weakens all of his minions. They can survive but are weakened, depending upon how many years they have behind them. They can gain strength by embracing others and becoming a creator themselves," he explains.

We spend the next few minutes putting the ashes of the destroyed *vampires* in silver boxes, the same way we did last time. Alexander takes care of burying the boxes to ensure there is no returning. He always wears the thick neoprene gloves when handling the silver boxes, so he isn't burned by the silver. I hope that maybe we can get Drake and Cyrus next time, the true leaders of the Cerberus.

Eliza approaches the rest of us, "I don't mean to break up the party, but we need to get to the manor and get the boys to the hospital. We still don't know if Isaac has been able to save the baby."

◆ ◆ ◆

Back at the manor, the boys all come running as we enter.

"Is everyone okay? Where is Mom and Dad, are they still with Isaac? Did any of the town's people see you? Or worse, did anyone get hurt?" Nathanial asks.

We all freeze, not knowing where to start.

"Let's sit down and we'll explain," Sophia suggests.

Eliza sits next to Luke and holds his hand, as Sophia does the same with Nathanial.

"Well boys, it was a difficult fight and a few of us got injured. We destroyed the leader and all those he brought with him. When we arrived on scene there was a car accident caused by the Cerberus. That is why Isaac is at the hospital," Florence explains.

"Oh lord, I hope the victims will be alright. Is it anyone we know?" Luke inquires, not suspecting what is about to come.

"Well that is where things are difficult. Yes, we all know the victims. I hate to tell you but it was your parents," Constance breaks the news.

Nathanial and Luke both jump to their feet, "We gotta get there now," Nathanial insists painfully. "Are they going to be okay?"

"Actually Nate, Luke, I hate to tell you this, but they did not make it. The Cerberus that caused the accident fed off them before we could get there," Constance continues.

We all watch as the two men who are like family to us, fall back to the couch and begin to cry for their parents. "Why, why them?" Nate sobs.

"I'm so sorry hon." Sophia cradles the man she loves so dearly as he tries to process the information.

"The baby, oh such an innocent little soul gone before it's time. He or she did not even get a chance to experience life," Luke cries even harder.

"Actually that's where there may be some good news," I insert.

"Good news, what could possibly be good about a baby dying before even born?" Luke defends.

"Isaac took your mom to the hospital for a caesarean section to try to save the baby. Your mom was gone, but I could still sense the baby. We don't know if Isaac was successful or not, that is why we need to get there now. If he was able to save the baby, the two of you will need to be there."

# CHAPTER THIRTY
## Trials and Tribulations

Once again we find ourselves walking through the front doors of the hospital to say
goodbye to someone we love. The elevator doors open and Isaac steps out.

"Come with me, we will talk in private," he says as he leads us around the corner. Isaac leads us to a large private waiting room that will fit all fifteen of us, the same one we sat in just one year ago.

As we take seats on the large couches and chairs, Isaac begins to explain to Nathanial and Luke. "When we got to the scene of the accident, Sophia realized it was your parents. We were able to get Nikole out of the car and Sophia tried to heal her. She soon realized that it was too late for Nikole, but the baby was still viable. I raced your mother here and performed a caesarean section to try to save the baby."

We can all see that the boys are destroyed. Luke fights through his tears. "You couldn't do it, could you?

It was too soon, Mom wasn't due for almost two months."

"I was able to save the baby. He is very small, but I have never seen a baby as strong as him," Isaac offers a glimmer of hope.

"He...we have another brother, and he is alive?" Nathanial says with complete surprise.

"Yes. Would you like to meet him?"

"Yes, of course. We're all that little guy has now." Luke jumps to his feet with a renewed sense of hope.

"It's okay Luke, I will go get him and bring him to you. He is so strong we don't even need to keep him in the nursery," Isaac says as he leaves the room.

Eliza and I try to console our boyfriends. We're all devastated over the loss. Mrs. McCord wanted another baby so badly, and now he is here, but she is gone. This seems like such an injustice. Yet the boys have composed themselves and like the men they are, become a new strength to their brother. Isaac then walks in with the baby.

"Nate, Luke, I would like you to meet your little brother." He pushes the basinet in front of the two brothers.

"He is so small. Are you sure he is alright?" Luke questions.

"Yes he is small, only four pounds. Although like I said, he is so strong. Most babies that are born almost two months before they are due suffer many complications. They have difficulty breathing, eating, they can have a hard time keeping their temperature and have heart defects, and the list goes on and on. I cannot understand why he is so strong. He is the healthiest baby I have ever seen, and there is no explanation," Isaac admits.

"Can we hold him?" Nathanial requests.

"Of course, I actually suggest it. One thing that is amazing for premature babies is called kangaroo care. This is where you place the baby to your chest, skin to skin. They absorb your warmth and hear your heart beat. It has proven to be miraculous in helping little ones progress."

Nathanial reaches down and picks up his new baby brother, "What are we going to call you little one?" he asks with tears rolling down his face. Only holding him for a moment, he places the baby back in the bassinet.

Luke looks at his two little brothers, "I don't know what Mom and Dad would have called him, but I think we should name him after Dad: Arthur."

"Don't you remember how much Dad hated his name?" Nathanial says with a smirk.

"Yeah you're right, I guess we have something to think about."

Everyone in the room forgets about our grief for a moment and takes in the beauty of the new life in front of us. Eyln starts to levitate and places herself in the basinet, next to the new life. She snuggles right next to him and goes to sleep.

"That is the sweetest thing in the world," I say in awe.

Matilda smiles. "If you only knew," she whispers.

"What do you mean by that?" Sophia snaps her head to look at her sister.

"We have another match. Elyn and the baby are soul mates. I would also have to assume that Elyn knows it too." Matilda laughs.

Pondering what will happen to the baby and what he will be called, I smile at my baby girl snuggling next to him.

"I got it: Nikolas Arthur. That way he has both Mom and Dad's name, but doesn't have the name Dad hated so much, every day." Nathanial suggests.

"That's the perfect way to honor Mom and Dad." Luke agrees.

Luke reaches down, placing his hand on the baby's head. "It is settled. You have some big shoes to fill, little Nik. Our parents were amazing people, and you now carry their names."

"This is really amazing, but getting back to Mom and Dad; how did they die? Was it from injuries from the car accident?" Nathanial wonders.

Sophia takes his hand, "Actually, the accident killed your father and only hurt your mom. The Cerberus attacked and fed off your parents. I could have Embraced your mom if I had been just moments earlier, but don't believe that would have been the best choice, even if it were possible. Embracing only works if the heart is still pumping, at least enough to circulate the vampiric blood and venom through the system. I believe they deserve peace anyways, and it seems they didn't suffer long."

"Thank you for that Sophia, I don't think they would have been happy as vampires," Luke admits.

Elijah and Florence share a look, and Elijah looks over at little Nik. "What did you say? One of the Cerberus fed off of Nikole."

"Yeah, he almost drained her dry. Sorry boy's, I don't mean to be insensitive," Sophia shares.

The eldest Pierce's begin to examine the baby, lifting his limbs and testing his strength. "Oh no, Florence do you think...?" Elijah slips.

"What, what is it. What is wrong with Nik?" Luke begins to panic.

"No, no, Luke, don't panic. The baby was in-utero when your mom was bitten. So the venom from the vampire that fed off her traveled through her system and crossed the placenta to the baby," Florence explains.

"So my baby brother is a vampire?" he panics.

"Not really; becoming a vampire is a two step process. First the victim needs to be bitten and infected with the venom. After that the victim needs to feed on vampire blood. This completes the Embrace, turning the victim into a vampire. Normally the venom would just pass through the system," she continues.

"So he will be fine then, as soon as the venom passes through him?" Luke confirms.

"Well, see, that is where there is a problem. Because Nik was born with the venom, it will stay in him forever now." Florence breaks the news. "It is part of his blood now."

Nathanial takes a deep breath. "So, what does this mean for our baby brother?"

Elijah sits in between the boys. "Now that Nik is infected with the venom, he will have all the attributes of a vampire, although he will still be human, and he will still age as a mortal does. He can still go out in the sun and do everything a mortal does. Nik will have all the powers of the vampire; speed, strength, increased senses, and healing. He will not have the thirst for blood, nor will he be affected by any of the things that affect vampires."

"So, isn't all this good? He will just be extra strong and healthy? Kinda like the best of both worlds," Luke asks.

"Well, yes and no; he will need to learn to deal with his powers. The extra sensory powers alone could drive anyone insane—now just imagine a little baby. We will need to take precautions and help train him. He will need to be around us, as only we will understand what he will go through," Elijah continues to explain, although I can tell he is holding something back.

"What? So you think he should live with you? But Nate and I are both in Boston now. Oh no, what about college? I can't handle this right now." Luke buries his head in his hands.

"Luke, we don't need to worry about everything right now. We will help you." Florence goes down to Luke's level and puts her arms around him.

"I need to get the baby back to the nursery for observation. He should be able to go home tomorrow. I will fast track the paper work. Ebony, Eliza, can you please do up a temporary spell to help subdue his powers and senses, please?" Isaac requests.

"Of course, we'll do anything to help. Elyn, it is time to say goodbye to Nik. You need to get out of his bed now." I say, reaching down to pick her up and hand her to Matt.

Eliza and I place our hands on little baby Nik; we ensure to leave his advanced health, and healing intact. None of us are sure what might happen to him if we bind that as well. He is so tiny and fragile, we can't risk anything happening to him. Isaac then takes Nik back to the nursery and Constance takes Nathanial and Luke to identify the bodies. We will take everyone back to the Pierce house for the night, just as we did one year ago when Grams passed.

# CHARLOTTE BLACKWELL

# CHAPTER THIRTY-ONE
## Aftermath

The next morning, while Luke and Nathanial sleep, the entire Pierce family sits to watch the news. We need to know what people saw last night and decide how to deal with it.

"Here it is—they are talking about the accident and attack," Danika announces.

I turn up the volume a little as the broadcaster speaks. "Last night the center of town was ambushed by a gang. Thanks to a group of local heroes that were brave enough to fight them off, we are safe again. None of the witnesses have been able to identify Wenham's hometown heroes, but we thank them for their bravery. It has been noted that the gang members dressed in gothic wear and acted like vampires; they were very intimidating to those who caught a glimpse of the action. Unfortunately, two of our most respectable citizen's were lost in the midst of the fight. Nikole and Arthur McCord, parent's to star football player Nathanial and star basketball player Luke, died from their injuries following a car accident cause by the riot. Both Luke and Nathanial McCord attend Harvard on athletic scholarships. Dr. Isaac Pierce was able to save the baby Nikole McCord was expecting later this year. We will announce funeral arrangements once they are finalized. To donate to the McCord Memorial fund, in order to assist in raising the baby now left without parents, please donate at the local commerce under the McCord name."

We look around at one another, surprised that no one saw or at least understood what they saw. Our secret is safe.

"Can you believe the wonderful things they are saying about the McCord's? It is so nice of them to start a memorial fund, in order to raise Nik. I love this town more every day, and hate to think we will have to leave soon." Sophia admits.

It isn't even noon yet, and there is a knock on the door. Matilda jumps up to answer as no one wants to wake the boys. We can all hear what is going on.

"Hello, how can I help you?" Matilda asks.

"My name is Vanessa Steel; my mother worked at the nursing home with Mrs. McCord. She was working last night and heard what happened. We went shopping first thing this morning, and got this parcel to help the McCord boys with the baby. She thought they may be here, or at least that you would be able get this to them."

"You and your mother are too kind. They are here but are still resting as it was a long night. Thank you so much," Matilda says.

"Please tell them if they need anything, we're here to help."

242

"Of course I will; I'm sure it will mean so much to them. Thank you again," Matilda says, closing the door.

She returns to the family room with a large parcel. "Do you think we can open it?" she asks.

"As much as we all want to know what is inside, I think we should wait for the boys." Sophia answers.

With heavy footsteps coming down the grand staircase, almost as though their hearts are dragging down behind them, the boys enter. "Wait for us to do what?" Nathanial asks while rubbing the sleep out of his eyes.

"Vanessa Steel stopped by with this parcel for you. She said her mom worked with your mom," Matilda explains.

"Wow, people are already sending things. I know Mrs. Steel and Mom were close, but to already have a care package." Nathanial says with surprise. "Well, go ahead let's open it."

Luke pulls at the tape on the top of the box, and slowly opens the flaps on the box. Looking inside, Luke starts to pull out various baby items from the box.

"I don't believe it; there's stuff for Nik, bottles, and diapers, blankets, everything. How did she know?" Luke wonders.

"Hon, it was all over the news today about your parent's death and Isaac saving the baby. The town has started a memorial fund to help with Nik." Eliza fills the brothers in.

"Oh, wow. I can't believe the town is trying to collect money to help with raising Nik. I really feel awful about taking hand outs from others. I know how meticulous Mom was about things. Mom and Dad have...I mean had...life insurance and retirement savings. I am sure that once things get organized, we'll be fine. I just still can't believe they're gone," Luke shares.

"We will give you the same offer as we gave Ebony and Eliza. We, the Pierce family, are here for you. No matter if your parents had insurance and such, we have plenty and will help you in any way that you need. Your mother and I became very close, and I promised her that I would always be here for you boys," Florence insists. "We can worry about the estate later."

Florence goes to the kitchen to prepare something to eat for the boys. We all fed earlier. She makes the most amazing meals from combining animal and donated blood. Today it was a blood porridge infused with cinnamon. I smell the French toast she is whipping up for Eliza and the boys. I realize that it is almost time for Elyn's lunch.

"Sorry, please excuse me; I need to get Elyn's lunch ready before she wakes from her morning nap."

"Of course Ebony, please do what you need," Elijah insists.

I join Florence in the kitchen while preparing a bottle and some Pablum. Normally she would still be on the young side (being only five months old) to have Pablum, but she is advancing so much faster than babies her age and the bottle just wasn't satisfying her any more. I decide to talk privately with my newest mother figure.

"Florence, what is going to happen to little Nik?"

"There is no need to be worried about him; we will help the boys through. I know their parents would want them to stay in college, which will be hard to do for two boys raising their brother. You should understand better than anyone the difficulty of raising a child when you yourself are still a child."

"Yes of course I do; both Matt and I decided it would be better to put school off until Elyn is a little older. I know that some people can do it, but I just don't understand how. As much as I love Elyn, I really wish Matt and I would have been more careful. She is meant to be my daughter, but I wish she had come at a better time. How are the boy's going to handle school and a newborn?"

"Ebony, Elyn is a blessing. As much as I too love her, I will never deny that it would have been better for you to have waited. As for Nate and Luke, this will be tough with Nik being what we call a natural day walker. He needs to be trained to control his powers, just as any new vampire does. We'll need to work something out with the boys, but I think Nik should stay with us. That way they can still go to school and we can train him."

I nod in agreement. "I too think that's best; I just don't know what they'll think of it."

Florence calls out, "Eliza, Matt, Luke, and Nate your French toast is ready."

As they all sit at the table Florence places the meal on the table for them to help themselves. I call out to Elyn and she levitates out of her playpen in the office to the kitchen and sits in the highchair.

"Ready to eat, my little peanut?" I ask, while buckling her in the high chair.

I know the pain that Nathanial and Luke are feeling. I only wish they could be as lucky as I was and have the ability to see their parents. Later today, they'll have to go to the hospital and pick up their new baby brother, while the rest of us guarantee there are no more Cerberus lurking around and figure out what powers, if any, we absorbed from the vampires we destroyed. When one vampire destroys another, they absorb the powers of the one they killed. Not all vampires possess powers, although several do, either natural or absorbed powers. Everyone already has some pretty cool powers, but it would be neat to gain some new ones too. I would love one like Elijah; he can absorb others powers for use when in their range. Matt and Eliza volunteer to watch Elyn, as well as take Nathanial and Luke to the hospital. This is going to be another difficult week and we'll need to work together.

# CHAPTER THIRTY-TWO
## New Beginnings

Weeks have passed since the Cerberus took the McCord lives, and we destroyed their leader. Elijah has contacted the Renata, and it appears that none of the original or stronger Cerberus are in our area. I wonder if Drake and Cyrus went away to lay low for a bit. Elijah was given forgiveness from the Renata for the great laws that we broke. We've even been given permission to continue with our mortal loved ones. I still don't understand how none of the town's people realized we were having a vampire and magick fight in the middle of town, but then Elijah explains that some of the more powerful Renata came to town, and compelled all those that saw the fight. I start to understand the true power behind the rulers of the vampiric law. I try to recall the six laws set out by the Renata that we are required to follow. Grabbing a pen and paper I start to write them out.

$1^{st}$ Law
The Conspiracy

Thou shall not reveal the nature of thy being to anyone.
2nd Law
The Empire
Thy Empire is thine own concern and no other shall interfere.
Only the leaders may intervene if rules are forsaken.
All others owe thee respect while in it.
3rd Law
The Ancestry
Thou shall only Embrace another with the permission of thine leader.
Until one's own Empire is formed and is released from thine leader.
4th Law
Accountability
Thou is responsible for thine creations, rule them in all things.
5th Law
Respectfulness
Honor one another's Empire.
Thou must be respectful to the ruler of another Empire.
6th Law
Destruction
Thou art forbidden to destroy another's Embraced,
The right belongs only to thine ruler.

I think these are all great rules to follow, and could help many others of our kind to live civilly.

"Nate, it is time for us to figure out what we are going to do. The dean called me yesterday and said he can't hold our scholarships much longer. He needs us to return to school," Luke says.

"So what are we going to do? We can take Nik with us, but the Pierce family needs to still work with him. But I don't think it is a good idea for both of us to leave him," Nathanial admits.

"I won't let the two of you throw away your chance at education. Matt and I made the choice not to go to college this year, in order to care for Elyn; we can help with Nik too. If you don't go back to school, I'm scared you'll never go back," I argue.

"Ebony, I don't want you to worry. I appreciate that you're willing to help us, but he is our brother, and he needs to be with family. Maybe one of us should stay behind to raise him," Nathanial suggests.

There's a large crash from the other room; we all jump up and run to see what the commotion is. When we get in to the library, we notice tons of books off the shelf and Nik's pacifier on top of the pile. Elyn is sitting in the playpen next to Nik, trying to calm him as he screams. Nathanial runs to his baby brother, and picks him up in an attempt to calm him.

"What the heck happened in here?" Eliza questions.

Alexander quickly joins us in the library. "It was Nik, his strength. The sheer force of throwing his pacifier across the room is the cause of this destruction."

"What do you mean, he threw his pacifier? Nik is only a few weeks old. He shouldn't be able to do that yet." Luke's concern grows.

"Normally you'd be correct, but because Nik is a day walker, things are a little different. His powers allow him to physically advance faster than a normal mortal baby. You have to remember not only is he mortal, but he is half vampire," Alexander explains.

"I guess we really are going to have to figure this out sooner than later. Nate and I aren't equipped to care for our little brother." Luke's stress becomes visible.

"Luke, I think you need to go back to school. I will talk to the dean and see if I can get my scholarship rolled to next year," Nathanial insists.

"Nate, I can't let you do this. Mom and dad would kill me, and you worked so hard for this."

"As did you, Luke. This is your final year. You need to complete it and graduate and then finish your masters. I can go to community college, for now, but the only way that we will be able to take care of Nik is for you to get a good job and have the ability to provide for him," Nathanial reasons.

Sophia, Alexander, Matt and I take the babies up to the family room, and allow the boys some time to discuss their options. In the family room, Alexander attempts to work with Nik telepathically. Because Nick is so young it's difficult for him to understand and Alex needs to implant the thoughts in his head. Elijah and Florence join us and we explain what's happening.

"This is going to be more difficult than we thought. We have never had to train a day walker before. We may have to call in reinforcements. I have some friends in the Renata that may be able to help," Elijah, shares his thoughts.

"It may be our only option. Maybe you should make some calls," Sophia suggests.

◆ ◆ ◆

Deciding not to worry about Nik until Elijah has contacted his friends, Alexander starts to question me about my dream visions again.

"Still having visions of *ghosts* and *angels*, Ebony?" he bluntly asks.

"Yeah, actually I've talked to a few of the *ghosts*. It turns out that they are victims of the supernatural, everything from warlocks and demons, vampires, black magic, you name it. The *ghosts* that are coming to me have all died from some form of supernatural evil."

"Do you know how to help them yet?" Sophia asks.

"It appears as though they are having trouble crossing over. I've helped a few already; they need to let go of the anger within them, and to be able to feel peace. Others need to make sure that their families can survive without them. It makes me happy to know that I'm able to help others go in peace."

"Do you have any more information on the *angels* yet?" Eliza wonders.

"I've been helping Ebony to learn as much as she can. We still can't figure out if they are trying to help us or warn us of something. And deep down, I have a feeling that a *nephilim* is around and nearing his or her eighteenth birthday," Matt explains.

"So the next thing we need to do is try and figure out who the *nephilim* is," I add. "I have also been practicing meditation and learning realm travel, in hopes that something will help lead me to the *nephilim*." I learned from the book of shadows that any witch can travel through the realms once they train themselves proper meditation. So I've been practicing; I always thought this was a power not a skill.

"So, if there is a half fallen *angel* and half mortal walking around, would that also mean that fallen *angel* is amongst us? If that is the case, is there a danger to the town's people?" Eliza questions him.

"I don't believe so. Matt and I have been trying to look at all of the adoptions in the area as well as single parents. More specifically single parents, because they would more than likely be the ones left to care for the child, and may even know what their child is. Anyone between the ages of seventeen and nineteen is on our watch list. I have also learned that they don't have to come from a fallen, any *angel* can have a child, it's just forbidden. I guess this proves no one is perfect."

Sophia paces the room. "And what have you found out so far?"

"Well there are only about ten people on our list so far that fit the requirements." Matt pulls out his list. "Do you recognize any of the names on our list? I know I do."

Nathanial and Luke join us. They both appear somber yet settled, as though they have come to a decision. We momentarily change focus back to them.

"So, have you guys come to a conclusion?" Eliza questions as she holds Luke in her arms.

"Well, I have agreed to go back to school and Nathanial will stay here to help the Pierce family with raising Nik." Luke says as he gives his brother a disapproving glance.

Eliza looks up at her boyfriend. "Why do I have the feeling there is more to it than that?"

In a sarcastic tone, Luke says, "Nate, would you like to tell them."

Nathanial smirks at his brother. "Thanks bro. I was telling Luke that I thought it may be a good idea for your family to Embrace me. That way..."

"You can stop that right now, Nathanial McCord. Why on earth do you think that Embracing you can fix everything? I thought you promised me never to bring it up again," Sophia says with such frustration.

"Sophia, I know that we have talked about this, and I know what I promised you. What you need to understand is that circumstances have changed. My little brother needs you, just as I need you, but he also needs me. If he is going to have to go through life being half vampire and half mortal, I think he should have family on either side. Luke will stay mortal. It only makes sense, since his girlfriend is mortal too; although a super powerful witch, she is still mortal. With me, the woman I love is a vampire; you, Sophia Pierce, are the only one for me and I want to be with you. We can't go on forever with you as a vampire and me as a mortal. You know this just as well as I do. I know this may not be the ideal situation, but it's something that'll workout for all of us," Nathanial argues.

Sophia is visibly upset over at Nathanial suggestion. "You know I don't like the idea of this. You have no idea what it's like to never grow old, never complete any one cycle of life. You're just always stuck as a teenager. Life never progresses; never changes and you can never really call any one place home."

"Are you telling me that your life has sucked for the last two years that you have known me? I understand how difficult it could be being alone; but Sophia, we have each other, and this way, we always will!"

As I listen to Sophia and Nathanial argue, I began to think about what my life is going to be, now that I too am a vampire. My daughter and husband are still mortal; one day, Elyn will be older than I am.

"Excuse me please, I am just going to the guest house for a bit, if you need me." I grab a glass of Florence's blood punch and head to the guesthouse to ponder my existence.

◆ ◆ ◆

Back at the guesthouse, I look around trying to find something to make this a positive situation. It's been almost six months since I've become a vampire, and I never really thought anything of it. As I listened to Sophia and Nathanial arguing about the repercussions of Embracing Nathanial, I can't help but wonder if anybody thought about my repercussions. Sophia has told me how hard it is to cry as a vampire, but right now I don't find it so hard; the tears are flowing freely down my face.

Matt comes racing in. "Ebony, are you okay? Why are you crying? The way you left had us all so worried. Alexander was trying to reach your thoughts. He said you were upset about something, but then he got blocked. It must be one of the new powers you absorbed."

"Everything is so wrong. Sophia is right–you and Elyn are going to age, and one day our daughter is going to be older than I am, because I'm eternally stuck at seventeen years old, and will never get older. One day, you won't want to be married to a teenager."

"Ebony, there something that I have to tell you, and I am not sure if I'll make things better or worse for you, but it is time for you to know."

"How could things possibly get any worse?"

"You don't have to worry about me growing older than you. I have completed all the guardian training I can as a mortal."

"Well, that's good, isn't it?"

"Well, it can be, yes. The next stage for me to complete is to transform into a guardian and complete my magical training with the great ones. The only way for this to happen is for me... for my mortal body to die," Matt explains.

"You're freaking kidding me...you're going to die? I can't do this on my own. When, how long do we have?"

"No one can tell; it usually happens within one year of mortal training being completed." He takes me in his arms, using his calming effect to help relax me.

"It's not all bad, Ebony. We won't be torn apart. Once my upper-level training is complete, they'll return me to you in my human form. Once returned, like you, I will not age. I too will never have a twentieth birthday."

# CHAPTER THIRTY-THREE
## Choices

I find myself scared everyday that I'm going to lose Matt. I know once he's done his training he'll return to me, but no one knows how long that'll be. I need my husband, and Elyn needs her father; what will we do without him? Thanks to Matt, I have finally found the *nephilim*, another thing I could have never done without him. I would've never guessed that there are two right under our noses. Wenham has both a good and a bad *nephilim*, and we know them both. It is up to Eliza and I to banish the bad or try to turn her to the good side, and then to protect the good. I've realized it's my powers that brought the *angels* to me. The *angels* want to conceal the *nephilim*; they believe it is dangerous to have them walking the earth—or at least some of them feel this way. I'm learning about the various kinds of *angels*, but it's hard because of the secrecy behind them. Some *nephilim* are allowed to continue with their life, while others are hunted for evil because of their powers. Then some of the really good-hearted ones are protected by an *angel* called

Katherine. She's one of The Twelve as we know them to be called. We don't know much about The Twelve and what they do, but I hope we can learn more. Katherine trains them to be what she calls venators daemonum, hunter of demons. Though she has trained a few, many more are out there that have yet to be found. It seems that they believe I have the power to help them, or something. We need to figure out why these *angels* are coming to me. Something about this doesn't seem right though. I guess I will figure it out someday. Today I'm visiting with my sister and we are trying to learn as much as we can. It feels nice to be at the manor with my sister, I miss it.

Eliza and I search the Book of Shadows for a way to correct this awful injustice. This world is filled with such evil and hatred that we can't afford to lose yet another good soul.

"So, have we figured out yet if the *nephilim* even know what they are yet?" Eliza asks as she continues to search the Book of Shadows for answers.

"I believe Mel knows; I always knew that bitch was evil." I smirk at the thought of what's coming to her. Karma is the best payback ever.

"And what about Ben?"

"He must know—he is almost nineteen. Matt and Nathanial have gone to spend the day with him in an attempt to get information."

Eliza laughs. "Like anyone can keep a secret from Nathanial. He is getting stronger at extracting information. Not one of us have been able to keep secrets from Nate—I doubt Ben will be any different."

We both have a good laugh about that fact. Sophia arrives at the manor; both Eliza and I can tell how upset she is.

"Hey Sophia, what happened, hon?"

"It has been a week since Luke returned to school, and Nate won't let up about me Embracing him."

"Sophia, nobody can make that decision for you. Although I will say this—when I first heard your argument about why Nate shouldn't be Embraced, I was devastated. I thought you were absolutely right for not wanting to Embrace him. My family was going to grow old without me. Nobody gave me a choice. It was done to save my life and make sure that my baby had a mother. I'm grateful that Constance was able to save me. Matt will soon become a guardian, and he will no longer age either. Once he returns, we can be happy together, forever, knowing that we look as though we should be a couple. Nate's made this choice of his own free will. He wants to be with you and be with his brother to help in raising him. If you Embrace Nate, the three of you will be like your own little family, with Nate as a father figure and you as the mother figure." I begin to pour my heart on to my sleeve.

"I never really thought of it that way Ebony. It still worries me because what is done is done, and there is no going back. I'm just not ready yet." Sophia admits to her true feelings.

Before long, Matt and Nathanial return with Ben. I can't help but wonder what will happen with Mel. When it comes to her, she will get her karma, threefold. She was always so mean to everyone, including me, because of my supernatural abilities, and now she will get what she deserves.

"Hi Ben, how have you been doing?" I ask with slight concern.

Ben walks over and greets Sophia and me with a hug. "Well, I must admit that it is nice to finally know what's happening to me, but it's still shocking. Who knew all this supernatural baloney actually existed? When things started to change my mom explained what she knew, but I thought she was going crazy."

Sophia smiles, "If you only knew it all."

"So how is it you are going to protect me from these arc *angels* or whatever they are?" Ben inquires.

"Well there are a few things that we can do; one is get your wings clipped. The other is to prove to them how good you actually are. There is also an *angel* that helps good *nephilim* by turning them into guards for other *angels*," I explain. "We are kinda flying by the seat of our pants here and learning as we go. The guardians are a much different type of *angel*, not *angels* from God or, arc *angels* and so on. So bare with us as it's all new to us too."

"And exactly how do we do that?"

"That we haven't figured out yet, but we will." I ensure.

We decide it is best if we go and take care of Mel first. Pulling out my old yearbook, I cut her picture out and take my pendulum in an attempt to scry for her. We're able to track her at her mother's boutique.

Entering the shop, it appears as though no one is there. I notice a few black feathers on the ground, and decide to follow them. On the floor behind the counter I see Mel in a pool of blood.

"She's over here!" I yell. "I think the *angels* beat us to her." I notice a large stab wound that looks as if from a sword of some kind; the wound penetrates right through her.

"I think you are right." Sophia agrees. "She's already gone. There is no life essence left."

"So what do we do now?" Ben questions with a hint of panic in his voice.

"Well first of all, I think we need to call 911," Nathanial suggests.

"Nate, why don't you do that? I'm going to collect these feathers. The *angels* don't want anyone to know about them. Maybe they should be a little more careful." Ben snarks.

After the police and ambulance arrive, we give our statements and are released go back home.

"You know what sucks most is that I didn't even get the chance to deal with her," I complain.

"Ebony, you are better than that, so stop it," Eliza orders.

"You're right, I'm sorry. I think I just need to relax a little."

Eliza wraps her arm around me, "Why don't you and Matt go to a movie? I'll watch Elyn for you."

"You sure you don't mind? That would be amazing."

Instead of returning to the manor, we drive back to the Pierce residence. Elyn will have her own bed and toys there. I run to my room and get changed for a night out with my husband.

♦ ♦ ♦

"I'm really glad we got a night out, just the two of us. It's been a long time since we've just gone out and had fun," I say as Matt drives us home.

"I agree, think we should do it more often…"

"MATT, LOOK OUT!!!" I scream with all my might, and grab the wheel, trying to turn the car out of the way of the oncoming semi truck headed straight for us.

The tires screech and the car swerves as he slams the breaks, but it's not enough. The truck strikes us right in the driver side door, flipping the car several times and throwing me out the window. My vampire abilities have left me unharmed, with the exception of a few minor abrasions. Once the car stops rolling, I run to check on Matt. The car looks as though it's been crushed by a trash compactor; Matt's arm is all I can see hanging from the window. Using all my strength, I try to rip the metal from the car. The metal flesh of the sedan begins to creek but the metal is twisted too much and I can't move it. My emotions take over and I can barely function any more, collapsing to the ground hysterically, crying. "No Matt, it's too soon, it's too soon." I bellow. The sirens from the emergency response vehicles wail through the air. The moon shines bright through a clear sky tonight, as I hold on to the only piece of my husband I can see. With his hand in mine I sob like never before.

"Matt, it's okay, help is on the way. Matt, honey, I'm not ready for this. You can't leave Elyn and me yet," I cry.

I see a great beam of light from the moon shine directly in to the small hole of crushed metal leading to Matt. I see an iridescent silhouette of Matt leaving the car and floating within the beam.

"I love you Ebony, I will be back one day I promise," his spirit says as he joins the great ones above.

A paramedic runs up to me, "Are you okay ma'am, are you hurt?"

"No, it's my husband, he's trapped in the car; help him. Please." I beg for help even though I know in my head they can't help him, but my heart doesn't want to let him go.

He waves over his partner, who takes me by the arm. "Why don't you come with me and my partner can work on your husband? The firemen will come and help get him out of the car. I need to look at you and make sure that you are not injured."

The rescue workers take me to the hospital, and behind me, Matt's body follows in a second ambulance. Isaac and Constance are both on duty and waiting at the emergency room doors. Constance quickly rushes me off to a private room, where most of the family is already waiting.

"Florence and Elijah have gone to get the Barton's; they should be here any moment."

Over the next few hours we go through the exact same motions that we have done so many times already in the past year. How much loss can one group handle? I

263

will be happy to never see this hospital grieving room again.

# CHAPTER THIRTY-FOUR
## Giving In

The Pierce family decides it will be better to move me and Elyn back into the main house, since Matt's passing. I know they are worried about me, but I can't worry about what's happened. I need to concentrate on the future, on him returning. We won't be able to have a life here in Wenham anymore. Everyone knows about Matt's death, and when he comes back, we will need to find someplace new to live. I can't believe he didn't even make it long enough to see Elyn's first Yule, our Christmas celebration, and her birthday.

Sophia comes into my room and sits on the bed next to me. "I made a decision, Ebony."

"Decision about what?" I ask, with little interest.

"About Nate; I'm going to do it. I'm going to Embrace him."

She sparks my interest with this revelation, "What made you change your mind?"

"In just over a year, we've lost your Grams, Mr. and Mrs. McCord, and even you; if it wasn't for

Constance Embracing you, Eyln wouldn't have her mommy. Now Matt is gone; I can't lose Nathanial. I can't stand to lose one more person that I love. He has shown me what it means to love and enjoy the life that I live. I thought Wenham was an amazing place to live, but although I've gained so much here we have all lost so much too." Sophia confesses.

"So what is the plan? Does he know, or when are you going to let him know?"

"I'm going to tell him tonight."

"And how do you know that you'll be able to resist feeding from him?"

"Because, he has donated some of his blood to Isaac and Isaac has been feeding it to me for months now. With us becoming closer, Isaac though it would be a good precaution. I've also bitten him before, during our first night together."

"I don't understand; why on earth are you guys doing that?" I ask with complete and utter shock. "I would have thought that would make you crave it more."

"We did it in order to ensure that I will be able to resist the temptation. That's how Caspian killed Daniella. They were in a moment of passion and he got too caught up in the moment and bit her. When making love, the act of biting completes the connection. I can't even explain what it's like, but it is the most amazing feeling. We share the physical connection and a complete and total emotional connection. You experience every feeling the other is having and vice versa; it is like enhancing the connection and experience. When he bit Ashley it was too much; Caspian wasn't able to stop, and I never

266

wanted to be in the same situation as him. Even with all we've been through I have to be careful, and that scares me."

"I think it may be a good idea to have the rest of us around, just to ensure that nothing happens."

"Agreed."

Later that night we all gather in the family room for Nathanial's Embrace. Nathanial removes his protection watch, and passes it to his brother Luke.

Eliza faces Luke and puts her hands on both shoulders, "Are you sure you want to stay for this?"

He nods. "It's not that I don't trust you guys, because I do. I need to be here, to ensure that both of my brothers are safe and that things don't get out of hand by accident."

Eliza and I prepared a freezing potion, in case Sophia does get carried away. We can throw at her and stop her from feeding any further.

"Okay sweetie, are you ready? I know I am." Nathanial says with a smile.

"Ready as I'll ever be," Sophia says as she takes his hand in hers.

Sophia closes her eyes, and we all watch as her fangs protrude from her mouth. Holding Nathanial's hand, she lifts his chin, bringing his neck closer to her mouth, and with one swift motion, she bites down. Nathanial jumps and moans at the pain as his blood flows freely from the wound, and trickles down his neck from the corner of Sophia's mouth. I can't help but wonder if it hurt the last time she bit him; adrenaline from having sex could have masked any pain. We can hear his heart race and pound harder, allowing the venom to enter his system. Alexander connects to Nathanial's thoughts, and we all hear him repeating to himself, 'Keep going, don't stop'. Sophia sits there with her fangs embedded in Nathanial's jugular. We all notice that she is not actually drinking much of his blood, but only allowing her venom to enter him. She soon releases and strikes at her chest with a sharpened nail to open a wound for Nathanial to drink from. She guides Nathanial's face toward the opening and he begins to drink from her. The Embrace only completes when venom and blood from the vampire enter and circulate in the mortal's system. He quickly takes a few more sips before her wound closes over; we all know he wants to ensure he is receiving enough. Sophia kisses him on the forehead and turns away, allowing herself to retreat back to her normal state before looking at him again. I look over to Luke to make sure he is handling the situation alright. He is visibly torn up over his brother Embracing, yet understanding is also drawn across his face. My heart goes out to these two men that are like family to me.

The Embrace is taking effect very fast on Nathanial; his wound is already healing. I can't help but wonder why it is happening so quickly. Alexander looks at me and says telepathically, 'Because she allowed so much venom to flow into him and did not remove much of his blood. It is able to flow through his system more freely and his blood supply doesn't need to replenish. This allows the Embrace process to speed up.' Florence sits next to Sophia and attempts to comfort her. The tears fill her eyes knowing what she has just taken away from the man she loves.

"Sophia my dear, he wanted this and it is for the best. The Oolatec clan from Transylvania will be here tomorrow. They will help both Nate and Nik get through this. The Renata said they are the best, and we do know them well."

"I know it's for the best, but it is still hard taking away every plan for the future and the life of the man I love."

◆ ◆ ◆

The following evening, there is a swift, sharp knock at the front door. I can hear Elijah greeting his old friends.

"Tryphosia, Azubah, it is great to see you again. Thank you so much for coming. Please come in." Elijah welcomes them.

"It is nice to see you again Elijah; two centuries is far too long to go without seeing friends," says the man.

"Yes, I apologize for that. I've been working on keeping a civilized clan."

A beautiful female voice that sounds like a musical instrument says, "We understand; it took us many years as well."

"Please make yourself at home; shall we take a seat in the family room? Florence will be out in a moment with some refreshments. She has done a wonderful job of increasing our meal choices."

"Thank you for your hospitality, but I would love to learn more about the day walker you said is amongst you," inquires the man I assume is Azubah.

269

CHARLOTTE BLACKWELL

"Of course, my daughter for all intents and purposes became involved with a mortal; his mother was with child, and was attacked by a member of the Cerberus. She died, but the venom was able to cross the placenta and infect the baby before he was born. He is now well over one month old; we call him Nik. Since both of the parents are gone, Nathanial decided it was best if he become one of us, and Sophia Embraced him, in order to care for the child. Nathanial was Embraced last night. Nik and Nathanial's oldest brother, Luke, has remained mortal. Since the baby is half vampire, and half mortal, the brothers felt it would be best to have one of each raising him."

"That is very unique and interesting story Elijah. We have dealt with half bloods, or day walker as you call him, in the past. We can work with both boys and have both trained within a week. It will be very difficult work for both of them," confirms the woman with an angelic voice.

"In a week, intense training? I can understand for Nathanial, but how is this possible for the baby?" Elijah shows some concern.

"I have power that is difficult to understand. I am able to transfer anything I have learned to another being. I am able to train others by implanting only the knowledge I wish for them to have. I leave out a lot of my past experiences, as well as my own personal experiences, giving them only what they need to successfully survive as a civil vampire."

"Azubah, that is the most amazing power I've ever heard of. I understand why you don't share what you can do with many. If any rogue vampires found out they would attempt to steal it from you."

"That is correct Elijah, and some have made their attempts. But none have succeeded. Shall we meet the boys and the rest of your clan?"

"Yes of course, but we consider ourselves a family, not clan."

"Our apologies, my dear friend," the woman says.

One by one, we file into the family room and Elijah introduces us. "You remember my wife Florence I assume? This is Isaac and Constance–they have been with us the longest and are like siblings to us. Both of them are medical doctors, and very talented. You wouldn't believe the work Isaac has done with blood and blood products, developing a new way for us to feed. He has used expired blood products from the blood banks to invent a synthetic whole blood. It is also currently in the testing phases with the FDA for medical use with humans," Elijah begins. "Next is one of our sons, Caspian. He was absent from the family for many years but has recently returned. Danika has been with us just over three years now. She was Embraced and left in the streets. We took her in, and just as with any teenage child we have dealt with her rebellion, but she is becoming a wonderful addition to our family. This is Matilda; we Embraced her in the early 1900's. She was being persecuted by witch hunters and our son Alexander knew he couldn't go on without her. That brings us to our twins, Alexander and Sophia. They were attacked by Cerberus in 1894 and left for dead. We Embraced and train them. Ebony has been with us for approximately six months now. Her and her sister are The Magnificent Ones, the witches born to help save the world. Constance Embraced her as she was dying from a medical procedure. Her daughter Elyn is also a witch, and her husband Matt just passed on and is completing his training to become a guardian. Elyn is staying with her aunt and Nathanial's brother for the night. Then of course, there is Sophia's boyfriend Nathanial, whom, as you already know, was Embraced last night, and this is his baby brother Nik, our little day walker."

"This is a very large coven or clan—no, pardon me, you call it a family. I am pleased to meet you all. My name is Tryphosia, and is my husband Azubah."

"Thank you so much for coming." Sophia shakes their hands.

We gather around, getting to know each other a little better. Eliza, Luke, and Elyn are all safe at the manor. I don't want to take any chances, having mortals around vampires that Elijah has not seen in almost two hundred years.

# CHAPTER THIRTY-FIVE
## Reflection

Things have been so crazy in the months since Matt's death, I don't know if I'm coming or going. I have to believe that he'll come back to me one day, and back to Elyn. His parents are so wonderful and encouraging. They too knew this day would come, but also hold on to the glimmer of hope that they will see him again soon. I sometimes think that Elyn sees him; she sometimes stares off in to space and lets out a huge smile and a giggle. I even swear that I heard her say 'dada' the other day. I guess it is possible; I can see *ghosts* and *angels*–it would only make sense that some of my powers transfer over to her.

I write letters to him telling him every milestone his little peanut goes through. That way when he returns to us, he will not have missed thing. Our friends the Williams are coming to see us today. Dakota and I have become good friends and it will be nice to see him again. We haven't seen the Williams since Matt's funeral; I haven't seen many people from outside the family since then. The family is trying to get me to interact with others. Florence has been concerned about me shutting myself off from others. I just wish they would understand that I need time; I lost my husband and my baby's daddy. Do they really expect me to just get over it?

Alexander walks in the room. "Ebony, I had to come and talk to you. We don't expect you to get over Matt; he was your soul mate, and who knows if you can ever find another? What we don't want is for you to sink in to a deep depression and shut us all out. It will make for a very long existence."

"I know, really, I do. It is just so hard Alexander; every time I look at my beautiful baby girl I see Matt, and I can't tell you how much I miss him."

"Kiddo, you don't need to tell me, I understand more than anyone. I want you to think of how Elyn has been lately. She is not her happy self, and that's because she feels your pain. We have to give her the best life we can until Matt can return to you. Hold on to that; he will return one day."

Alexander is right; I am not accomplishing anything, except hurting my little peanut. Her empathy skills make it so she feels every bit of my pain and anguish. I'm not being fair to her; no baby should feel this kind of heartache. I decide today is a new day. I'm going to start enjoying my life...existing with Elyn and helping her enjoy her life. I get up, hug Alexander and whisper, "Thank you." I guess now is a good time to rejoin the land of the living and the un-dead.

♦ ♦ ♦

Outside in the garden, the rest of the family is enjoying their visit with the Williams family. The garden is a lovely place to relax; there is the perfect amount of shade and a beautiful gazebo. Matt and I had the perfect wedding here just last year, and I've decided to hold on to the wonderful memories like that. Elyn and Nik catch my attention, playing in the play yard together. Nik is still young, but his strength as a day walker has allowed him to learn to sit at less than two months old. I'm still amazed at the training Elijah's friends were able to give both him and Nathanial. We thought I progressed quickly; Nathanial was able to go out in public after two weeks. He's even taken a job working for Elijah at the law firm and signed up for distance learning to become a lawyer as well. I know that makes Sophia happy, as she was concerned about him losing his ambition.

Dakota runs up to me and wraps his dark muscular arms around me. I bury my head in his chest and take a few cleansing breaths to calm myself. I've always felt a closeness to Dakota; it is nice to have a friend that I don't have to see or talk to daily, and yet we still remain as close as ever. "Hey there pretty mama, how you doo-in?" He smiles as I look up into his chocolate brown eyes.

"Better, thanks to Alexander." I smile over to my new brother. "How are things going with you? Notice any more creepers?"

"Creepers?" he give me a what the...look.

With a giggle I say, "Yup creepers, that's what I've decided to call all the evil entities now. They just creep on in where they're not wanted."

"Well Ebony, that's why we came today," Dakota announces, and the others all stop to listen.

"Aw man, don't tell me we got more problems. I am so not in the mood to deal with these creepers today," I start to whine.

"No, no, don't worry that perfect little head of yours."

"So, then what's going on Dakota?" Matilda inquires.

"Well, Dad and I've been talking to the elders, and we all agree that the supernatural activity in and around town has been increasing at an alarming rate. I mean, for the longest time it was just us shifters and a few wannabe witches. Now of course we had no true knowledge of your family."

"I agree, but I'm not sure I understand what you're getting at."

"Well, now with shifters, witches, vampires, demons, vampire cults, and nephilim, well we think..." he looks around at the others watching his every move, "that we should have some kind of full time training. We need to learn if there's any more of our kind and train them as well, before it's too late."

"Okay, I think I get it, like an after school program for the supernatural?"

"Not an after school program, my dear," Tamo cuts in, "A full time program; we could even find those from other areas and have it like a boarding school. The students will still be required to complete their state curriculum, but they will also do magickal or supernatural studies."

276

"Tamo, this is an amazing idea!" Florence beams with sheer elation.

"Do you really think we will find teachers that will want to work at a school for the supernatural's of the country?" Danika questions.

Dakota smiles. "That is where we come in lucky. See, Skah and his new wife are both educators. They met in college and married this past month. Now that is a whole other issue, the bugger eloped and we couldn't throw them a proper ceremony. She's nice, though, and minored in mythology, so she is very understanding and knowledgeable of the supernaturals of the world."

Elijah walks up and down the cobble stone path; we can all tell he is contemplating the idea. "I think it is a wonderful idea. I will contact the Renata to make sure they approve of us participating and then we can work out the details. I even have an idea for a location."

"Superb my friend, we will let you be to attend to your arrangements. We can talk more once you have approval." Tamo shakes Elijah's hand and the Williams proceed back to their reserve.

I have a great feeling about this school and can't wait to share it with Eliza. At last a place where others like us can come, learn and feel comfortable; a safe place where we can all work together for the greater good of man. Eliza and I can perfect our powers.

CHARLOTTE BLACKWELL

## About the Author

Charlotte Blackwell is the talented new Canadian author of the Embrace Series. She is someone to keep an eye on for years to come, with her unique voice and way of connecting with the readers, Charlotte is bound to be a house hold name for years to come. During her younger years Charlotte was friendly and outgoing, but never really voice her opinions and felt more comfortable falling behind the shadows of those around her. Something she hope to help others avoid. She began writing as a way to express her feelings, without having to confront those around her. As Charlotte grew and had a family of her own, she learned the importance of standing up for what you believe in and always staying true to one's self. Then one day the writing took over. Charlotte soon realized through writing she could combined her love for the paranormal and her children. Using writing as an outlet to reach out to those she cares most about, her children. Knowing the difficulties teens face, she wanted to use her stories to help her daughters understand they are not alone and now hopes to help others receive the message as well. Through doing this Charlotte discovered herself and with her husband and three children couldn't have written a happier end for her family.

## The Embrace Series

## Look for Book 4 Coming Soon

# Other books available from World Castle Publishing

### The Crossroads Saga by Mary Ting

### The Children of Nox by Joann H. Buchanan

### Desire Everlasting by Karen Fuller

CPSIA information can be obtained
at www.ICGtesting.com
Printed in the USA
LVOW12s1536190416

484331LV00002B/404/P